# BILLY O'CALLAGHAN

Billy O'Callaghan is the author of the critically acclaimed novel *My Coney Island Baby*, which has been translated into nine languages. His story 'The Boatman', which is collected here, was shortlisted for the Costa Short Story Award. He lives in Douglas, a village on the edge of Cork City.

ALSO BY BILLY O'CALLAGHAN

Story Collections

*In Exile*
*In Too Deep*
*The Things We Lose, The Things We Leave Behind*

Novels

*The Dead House*
*My Coney Island Baby*
*Life Sentences*

BILLY O'CALLAGHAN

# The Boatman

## And Other Stories

VINTAGE

1 3 5 7 9 10 8 6 4 2

Vintage
20 Vauxhall Bridge Road
London SW1V 2SA

Vintage is part of the Penguin Random House group of companies
whose addresses can be found at global.penguinrandomhouse.com

Copyright © Billy O'Callaghan 2020

Billy O'Callaghan has asserted his right to be identified as the author
of this Work in accordance with the Copyright, Designs and Patents
Act 1988

First published by Jonathan Cape in 2020
First published in Vintage in 2021

penguin.co.uk/vintage

A CIP catalogue record for this book is available from the
British Library

ISBN 9781784708757

Printed and bound in Great Britain by Clays Ltd, Elcograf S.p.A.

Penguin Random House is committed to a sustainable future for our
business, our readers and our planet. This book is made from Forest
Stewardship Council® certified paper.

For Irene,
who always thinks I'm better than I am.

# Contents

# The Border Fox

The fields were sodden from four days of late-February rain and the cold dawn air smoked to every torn breath. We'd been moving across fields for upwards of an hour and had now lifted our pace to a half-run; four of us, dressed in denim jeans, thick sweaters and coats, each man spread out from the next by a span of thirty or forty paces. Now, finally, an unseen sun had begun to feather the sky's easternmost fringes. We'd quickened to a run because time mattered, and because we all sensed that the border had to be close; and with dawn breaking, these were the dangerous moments.

I had the right flank. I was seventeen years old, and tired and cold after a long night, and this was my first time over the border into the North. I had spent years listening to the stories that my father and brothers liked to tell, and to the songs they'd sung, but the past ten hours had been another kind of reality, and very different from what I'd imagined. Arriving at dusk, standing in a copse of ash trees with Larry Burke, Sean Crowley, and five strangers holding machine guns and whose eyes never

1

stopped studying me, trying hard to look comfortable in my silence after Dan Stoute, an uncle on my mother's side and our man in charge, had been led out of sight by a couple of other armed men so as to receive further instructions. Later, sitting by a turf fire in the busy upstairs room of an Armagh village pub that we'd accessed by a concealed back stairway, waiting for the rawness of those woods to leave my bones and swallowing from a pint bottle of tepid Guinness while people talked at me in accents so thick I could make out barely one word in six. Old yellow and brown daffodil-patterned paper cloaked the walls, the linoleum-covered floor wore a skin of fresh sawdust, and an unseen transistor radio, tuned through mists of static to Radio Éireann, hummed soft airs played on fiddle and banjo. And from the room's far corner, a girl of about my own age, a beautiful creature with gatherings of coppery hair and a flimsy white blouse burnished by the glow of the nearby kerosene lamp, sat on a low stool with her legs crossed tightly at the knee and kept making apparently accidental eye contact with me and smiling.

It's possible that places wear different faces for different people, but that was the Ulster I'd found, that and running through these muddy fields, trying to make the border with dawn still just a suggestion and then a softness in the sky. I ran in line with the others as the night around us lessened, and clambering over ditches, wading through gullies and once, up to my knees almost, through a stream bulked by all the recent rains, decided that this land, away from the accents and the tension pressing every surface, could easily pass for Cork or Kerry. There was the same cold freshness, the same field and ditch details – bracken, furze, the swathes of clawing bramble, the scarlet-berried rowan trees – that I knew by heart from mornings out with the hounds on a drag hunt or with the terriers in chase of rabbits. Land partitioned and labelled British, but Irish to its very soil.

Pat, my eldest brother, had given me the word. Something to be delivered, an easy job for a first outing. Think of it as training. And I'd be in good hands; the other three knew the run of things. 'Don't ask,' he said, when I had enquired, just between brothers, about the parcel. 'The less you know, the less you'll be able to tell, if the wrong people get a hold of you. Best for everyone, that way.'

At the safe house in Armagh, we'd split into pairs and were driven in two cars, staggered by twenty minutes, to a rendezvous point on the outskirts of Newtownhamilton. From the few words that I had picked up and pieced together, our parcel was destined to be tucked under a chair at an Orange Order meeting in Crossmaglen, either the following Saturday night or the one after, depending on who'd be in attendance. The precautions were routine, but deemed militarily necessary. Because, up here, mistakes were punished hard and there was no room for second chances.

'An hour to the border,' Dan Stoute had told us, after we'd watched the second car's tail lights make red eyes in the distance and then vanish, taken by a bend in the road. And another hour, more or less, after we'd crossed back over into the Republic, to the friendly farmhouse this side of Castleblayney. We'd get breakfast there, and a chance to revive ourselves by a roaring fire, and transport would be standing by to take us back down to Cork. Once we were across into Monaghan, he said, we could stop and rest a while if we needed to, but because of all the recent activity, and because of the massive incendiary device that had been discovered, a month or so earlier, just before it could take the walls and upper floors off the barracks at Newry, the RUC were on heightened alert for movements anywhere along the border. It was unlikely that the patrols would be out here, but it still paid to be vigilant.

The way he'd talked made the crossing sound like nothing at all, but his words hadn't taken the cold of the morning into consideration, or how the soft, stultifying fields pulled at every step until it was like wading in the sea, turning four miles into the equivalent of twenty and putting lead in every pocket. Now, an hour in, and the border was somewhere among these fields or patches of woodland, the uneven ground divided along irregular lines by centuries-old ditches or briar-clad stone walls. And even when, somewhere behind the cliff-sides of further rain cloud, a winter sun began to drag itself into the sky, my mind was bound fast to the ache in my knees and thighs and the inferno that had engulfed my lungs. I kept going, because what mattered was getting clear. As badly as I hurt, I still felt reassured by the presence, whenever I glanced leftwards, of the accompanying silhouettes. Sean Crowley, the nearest man to me, was close to fifty years old and badly out of shape, and I could hear the rasp and squeal of his breathing even from thirty, forty yards of distance.

I'd begun to crawl up over the next of the uncountable shoulder-high ditches, and was still looking across at Sean and at the lightening backdrop, when a shot rang out. At first, confused, I couldn't place the sound's origin, though it seemed impossibly close, and I glanced stupidly skywards, because something had gone past my face in that direction hard enough to move the air. Behind it, almost separate, the sound came, the sharp crack, in the same instant there and gone, leaving behind a dawn of great stillness, as if the very world had shuddered to a halt.

Instinct took over. I lurched on, scrambling up through the bramble and trying to kick away the tendrils of briar that snagged at my ankles, but just as I reached the top of the ditch, something bit at me. I felt a small slam against the underside of my right wrist and in the same instant a second shot sounded, again close enough to feel its jarring reverberation, the sound of someone putting a hobnailed boot-heel to a held-down forearm, that dry crunch of a bone being broken clean, but with the sort of inner loudness that far exceeds the reality.

And then, as I cleared the ditch's brow, something moved in the long grass down below. I didn't hesitate. My pistol was in my hand, cold and heavier than I'd remembered, and I straightened my left arm and squeezed the trigger, once and then, in quick succession, twice more. And then I was over, leaping down into the next field, my weariness forgotten now, obliterated by a white heat.

I threw myself to the ground, as I'd been trained to do, but the shooting was done. Still I lay there, my lips whispering frozen breaths that fogged the dim quarter-light, blurring everything. The grass had a clean, wet smell from all the recent rain, but the earth beneath tasted of sourness and stone, ripe with all the dead there's ever been.

I could tell that time was passing by the hard beating of my heart, the feel of it like a pain, thick and bitter, high up in my throat. But whether that accounted for seconds or minutes I couldn't have said. Instead, my mind busied itself with the sudden memory of a fox I'd once seen, during a drag hunt, running in a wide sweeping arc across a bright frost-covered hillside, ahead of a pack of hounds already weary from five or six miles of hard chase. The rust-flash of its body held like firelight against the blue-white landscape, the outstanding colour in the day, and I'd been young but not so young that I couldn't sense the transcendence of the moment, the raw and terrible beauty of nature at full stretch. And in the upstairs of the pub, only hours earlier, the girl had shone in much the same way, lustrous and as wild. Campfire embers. She'd watched from across the room, knowing from the overheard whispers who I was or was trying to be, why I'd come here and what I had committed myself to do; and her smile, when she caught me looking, had the flashing dance of that fox in full flight, a high breathless thing, alive with the terror of its own tease.

'Séamus!' someone called out in a loud whisper from behind the ditch.

I raised myself from the ground and discovered that I was still holding the gun. Blood poured in gouts from my right wrist, but I felt no pain yet.

After a couple of seconds, Sean Crowley came into view, walking at a stoop and trying to keep close to the cover of the ditch in case there were other snipers lying in wait.

'You're hit?' he asked. Then, almost in the same moment, he saw how my hand was hanging, dropped to his knees beside me and began swabbing at the wound with tufts of long grass. Blood continued to seep in black pulses, and he popped the button of my shirt's cuff, pulled up the sleeve and gripped my forearm tightly. Almost at once, the haemorrhaging slowed.

The others came, Larry Burke trying to watch every direction at once, though there was nowhere near enough light yet in the morning to see very far; and some moments after him, Dan Stoute. 'How is he?' Dan asked, his voice more curious than concerned.

'He'll need to get the arm tied,' Sean said. 'The bullet went clean through and must have caught a vein. He's losing a lot of blood.'

Larry began to unbuckle the leather belt from his own jeans. 'Will this do?'

Sean nodded that it would, and took the belt and tied it in a simple knot around my forearm almost to the elbow, tightening until I grunted in discomfort. We watched the wound bubble, then run slowly clear to reveal a gaping hole.

'Can you stand?'

'I'm fine,' I said, when I saw how they were looking at me. Murmuring the words, not trusting the strength of my voice, I got unsteadily to my feet. 'It's nothing. I'll be grand.'

They all recognised bravado, but needed to believe me. And to spare me further scrutiny, they turned back towards the ditch. The RUC officer lay in the field's gully, partially covered in the long grass, only the deep seaweed green of his sodden uniform and the wan three-quarter moon of his face in semi-profile interrupting the nature of the scene. With no wind, birdsong filled the morning, the high plaintive chatter of robins and linnets in the nearest trees, punctuated by the driving flute notes of a blackbird somewhere very close by.

'Christ,' said Dan, after several seconds had passed. 'He was lying in wait. He must have been patrolling this stretch and heard us coming.'

'Why is he alone, though? That makes no sense. Shouldn't there be others? Shouldn't we be buried in the ditch there, trying to gun our way through an entire regiment?'

Dan looked at Sean, and then back down at the body. 'Who knows? But we're talking more than two hundred miles of border between Warrenpoint and Derry. That's a lot of ground to guard, especially with any one of the towns and villages along the way, on either side of the line, liable to light up at half a minute's notice.'

'Poor bastard, all the same,' said Sean.

'He knew the score.'

'I doubt he knew he'd be signing up for this, having to spend his nights out here, alone and miles from anywhere friendly. How did he think it'd play out? He was always going to be outnumbered, and even if he managed to get one or even two of us, the odds still wouldn't have been doing him any favours.'

Larry spat on the ground. 'We have hundreds of our lads locked up, Séamus's father included, and Christ only knows the kind of beatings they have to bear. And think of all the women widowed and children orphaned. Save your pity for our own people.' He paused, and spat again. 'I say, fuck this one. Let the crows have his eyes and I hope the rats make a nest of his arsehole. A bed in hell to him.'

'He wanted us dead,' said Dan softly. 'That's the fight. Like I said, he knew the score. War is not a game.'

I stood beside the others and heard their words, but from a distance. I didn't want to look at the body, but had to, because this was too much of a thing to be forgotten or denied. I'd fired three shots from almost touching range. All three had hit. And that's how easy it was to kill a man, to destroy a life and maybe other attached lives, too. Because no man is ever truly a man alone. A heart had stopped beating because of me. Lungs had ceased taking air. And somewhere, at some hour of this day, other hearts would twist in pain in response to the news of what had happened here. The eye visible to me because of the head's partial turn stared widely, still full of glimpsed horror and gleaming like rain on glass. Inches down the face, one of my bullets had opened a crater that decimated nose and upper lip to white shards of bone among the deeper pulp. The lower jaw protruded, exposing a row of perfect teeth and offering the worst imaginable half of a terrible grin. And as I watched, the white of the eye began to fill with blood.

'The bastard asked for it,' I muttered, and the words were like a foreign language in my mouth. The air inside them quivered. 'And he shot first. What else could I have done?'

'You did well, boy,' said Dan, putting a big hand on my shoulder. 'Better him than you. Keep telling yourself that. And he's one less for our lads to worry about.'

'There'll be hell to pay when they find him.'

Dan shook his head. 'No, there won't. They'll do well to find him at all. And if it goes more than a couple of weeks there won't be much to find. But they'll get the message, soon enough. They drew the border line, not us. We're the ones who belong. But there'll be time for talk later. We need to be moving. It's getting bright, and the noise of the shots will have carried a fair distance at this hour.' He looked at me again, at the way I was cradling my right arm with my left hand, then turned away and started westward out across the fields in the direction of Castleblayney. Larry hesitated only a second before following, and then Sean and I began to move, too. Not speaking, not looking at one another, just walking, and trying hard to resist the urge to look back.

In the days and weeks that followed, I tried to avoid newspapers and radio broadcasts. The body had been found and identified, and for a while I carried the name with me, until others replaced it, and until time made it seem less than it was. People looked at me differently, the ones who counted, those who knew and who knew what it was like; and around me there was a new kind of silence, as if we had all somehow moved into a place beyond words. Everyone is marked in permanent ways, and those marks might make us ugly to some eyes but they don't stop us from living.

I've been to the North on several occasions since but, when I think about that first time, my clearest recollection is of how the girl's hair had shone, the same way tree sap does in sunlight. And I remember how her smile had at once excited and troubled me, perfect and wide over perfect teeth yet still somehow only half a thing, lingering only around her mouth. Her eyes were green and daring, young as spring but somehow full of winter, too knowing of long nights.

We'd meet again some months or a year later, in a cottage in south Armagh that was being used to house some visitors. I woke before dawn, rose and dressed while the others around me slept, and came through into the kitchen to find her buttering soda bread in front of a large window. She'd told me the night before, handing me a mug of tea, that her name was Siobhán, but with her accent she couldn't pronounce it the same soft way we did in Cork; and when I used it now, from the doorway, low with awareness of the early hour, she turned as if she'd been expecting me, and smiled the smile I'd so remembered. My wrist by then had healed as much as it ever would, but I'd slipped into the habit of touching it in times of stress, protecting it, and her eyes followed the movement of my hands and stiffened. She knew; everyone knew. She pulled out a chair from the table, and, afraid of how my voice would sound or what I might say, I simply nodded and came to sit. While a large kettle steamed slowly towards a boil on the range, she held herself close to me and examined my wound with her fingertips. I leaned back in my chair, matched her smile and surrendered myself to the coldness of her touch. And when she was certain that we wouldn't be disturbed, that we had time yet before the others stirred, she took me by the hand and led me outside, into the yard and then the back field, so that we could be animals together, red and wild.

# The Boatman

Margaret's brother arrives a little after four, coming up the yard in that lumbering way of his, still with sleep on him and hauling two shovels and a pickaxe, his boots on the gravel as familiar to me as the sound of my own voice in my head or my boat on the water, its old wood moaning among the waves.

I remain at the kitchen table, with a small glass in front of me and a refilled bottle beside the flat of my left hand. These past two nights have done for the whiskey, and I am reduced now to more home-grown poisons. But that's all right; we all have hard tastes here, and we're well used to the fire. From where I sit, I can see the staggered silhouettes of ash trees standing dense against the horizon. I drain the glass and pour again, running the alcohol to its brim, the liquid clear and illicit and full, for now, of the early hour, then slide it across the table in anticipation of my brother-in-law. A minute passes, the clock dropping its seconds in clicks, and if Michael seems to linger outside longer than usual I know that it is because he's looking at the sky, the stars, and listening for the first strains of birdsong. Savouring a rare morning without breeze.

When he enters, his steps trying to go gentle across the hall's linoleum, some of the house's inner balance shifts. After a moment he fills the doorway and leans against the jamb. Neither of us wants to speak yet, lacking I suppose the necessary words, but also because there's little left to say apart from expressions of anger, and we're both too beaten down for that. I gesture towards the glass, and he takes a couple of paces forward, picks it up in his thick fingers and drinks slowly. I watch him, then help myself to a last long, deep swallow from the bottle.

'Is herself asleep?' he says, and I nod. They'd given her something to put her down, because after so many days awake she was out on her feet. Now the house around us feels like a hole. She has fallen in and is still falling, and I am clinging to an edge. Everything that has gone before seems redundant now, all the efforts at survival, the love, the wasted laughter. Beth has cleaved us entirely open in her going. Without her, Margaret and I are nothing but collections of bones, emptied of worth. All I've wanted, ever since the hospital had first admitted her, was to be able to sit by myself and cry. But I am twenty-eight years old and haven't spilt a tear since I was a boy, and it seems that I have lost the ability to let go in that way. Margaret weeps, haemorrhaging tears almost, but I can only stand there, helpless, not looking at her but neither looking away. If I was a better man I'd take her in my arms and hold her, to feel her hair unkempt in my face and eyes, and her cheeks wet against mine and hot with fever, and to know the broken-hearted heave punching through her thin body. But that's still a step beyond what I can manage. I want to be strong for her, and we both know that it's what she needs and probably what I need too, but words of comfort are stuck in my throat. We're deep in this together, and yet the world feels untouchable around me. It's as if I've been set down on a jut of reef in the middle of the sea, some small hard rock with bottomless water a step away in every direction, and there is nothing I can do but stand and watch while others around me struggle to stay afloat and while my betters sink and drown.

Outside, at this hour, I know the morning well. Usually, if I haven't already cast off ahead of threatening rain, I will be loading my boat for the day. Four is not early for me. But this morning, because we are walking into instead of away from the dawn, up the hill to the old graveyard instead off towards the shore, I see the hour in a fresh way, blushed with new colours and bearing a different burden of darkness. When I lift my head, stars come up over the brow of the hill and, as we climb, are lost and the sky in that direction melts and turns a shade of blue that seems to soften with every step, every breath.

'You'd have thought the doctors could have done more,' Michael says, and his stare finds his feet in embarrassment at having spoken a private thought accidentally aloud. I listen to him as we walk, his exhalations making the sound of pages being turned. He has the pickaxe slung over his right shoulder. I am carrying the shovels. 'She was only young,' he adds, when he can't stop the rest from coming, 'and she didn't even seem that bad. A cold, maybe. But nothing worse than flu. How could it have already been too late? How were we supposed to know?'

I don't begrudge him his grief, even though it challenges my own in scale. Michael and Beth were close, not just uncle and niece but friends. He's like the rest of us in almost every way, but a part of him has remained relentlessly childlike. Maybe because he has never married. I suppose that's what put him always at such ease with her. He'd act the fool for her in ways that I couldn't, and was never short of time to spend on games. I did what I could, and Beth and I laughed plenty when we were together, but my duty was to work, and to provide. I've never had Michael's freedom, but also never wanted it. And other than that, we are the same. Cut from the one cloth. He is older than me by a few years but that doesn't matter in the least, and his hair where it has been cropped nearly into his skull at the sides of his head is already showing flecks of grey. Early thirties is snugly middle-aged here, especially on men. By then our skin has already tightened into the bones of our faces and our bodies across the shoulders and chest have set wide and strong. From hauling nets and turning earth. And we speak sparely and in a raw hush, having grown used to bending beneath the wind.

'They weren't blaming us,' I tell him, my voice low. 'It was no one's fault.'

'No,' he says. 'But she was only young.'

We follow the road up the hill, unhurried against the incline, and it feels as if all the weight of the world is on us, pressing us down. There's a chill in the air but we are both used to it, and it fills our mouths with something better than talk and freshens our minds. Ten or fifteen minutes later, we reach the graveyard. The side gate opens just enough for us to pass through, fanning into a rut in mud that has been parched by a fortnight of dry weather and westerly wind. Knowing the way even in the dark, I lead us among the slumped headstones and through long, stringy wisps of footpath grass towards the east wall, back to where the older graves lie. My thoughts are full of my father, and of the day we buried him, how the light had been, the peppered light of dusky, wet October, with a wind that diminished the priest's murmured prayers to mere mime. I remember the sensation of my tears squeezing from some tight place, but not spilling, even though I wanted them to, and how it had hurt to swallow when the time came for us to lower his coffin down into the dirt. For others, friends, relatives, men and women who'd known him all their lives, it was part of the ritual, that shining pine box the closing down of an existence, another dropped stitch in the tapestry of our island; but my mind was full of the man himself, the person I'd loved most in the world from before I even had any idea of what the word meant. And it was not so easy to let go. I could feel him there with me, by my side and all around, and I didn't need to see to know his face, his stories, his heart. Such details were burnt into me.

Now, at his graveside all these years on, I pick open the buttons of my shirt and strip to the waist. The dark has thinned around us and the cold feels good against my skin after the uphill walk. Michael watches me in silence, then steps back a few paces, understanding how much room I need, and I move into place, heft the pickaxe high above my right shoulder and begin to attack the dirt.

I have always enjoyed reading, but it is a pleasure that has deepened in recent years. Sleep comes hard for me; if I can get three hours then I'll count that as a decent night. So, after Margaret has gone to bed, and so that I won't disturb her by burning a light, I'll sit up in the kitchen and for a while get into a book, in order to put myself down. I've lived this way since before we were married, and I always have an old paperback in my pocket. It's about filling the spare moments, I think, blocking out the spaces between acts. Sometimes, when I am out in the boat and after I have cast my nets, there'll be a period of calm, and I'll have a chance to sit a while and simply watch the sky, to enjoy the flashing colours of the light on the water, and to ponder. Summer days start early, and two or three miles out to sea the only sounds to be had are often those of the gentle swell lapping at the sides of the boat and maybe the occasional screech of a gull or gannet or the splash of something missed by the eye breaking the surface for air before going back under.

I'll breathe then and look up from the page, and in the same moment I'll feel at home and violently dislocated because my mind has its own way of lingering in far-off lands. A thousand stories crowd my head, maybe a hundred thousand, and I understand if I think about it that I've made worlds of the places in which those stories play out every bit as much as their creator has; I've flushed them with the reek and music of life, I've filled them with voices. My Texas Panhandle, my Tartar Steppe, my Society

Islands exist for me as vividly as they will for those who have actually felt the grass and dirt of such places beneath their feet. Thoughts like that flip daily living into the chaos of a spinning coin so that in the same instant everything is true and nothing is. Our surroundings are there as we perceive them, and our dead are at once gone and everywhere.

As I age, I find myself favouring novels and stories that I know will end happily, not because that makes them more believable but because the very inverse of that is true, because their sense of reality softens and they again get to be something more than the world as it has shown itself to me. Not bad all the way to its core and rarely intentionally so, not without its beautiful moments, but neither naturally set up, it seems, for happy endings. Because in the end there's always death, and always broken hearts. Happy stories, at least, get to hold the air of magic.

Some years back, I read something about a Chinese boatman that made a deep impression on me. Since then I've thought of it often, sitting out in my own boat on silent mornings, and it has been a constant in my head these past few days, though I can't recall its title or whether it was even a story or a novel. It retains the scope of a novel for me, and yet I seem able to sum up what little plot there was in a few brief sentences, understanding of course that, sometimes, plot is the very least of what constitutes substance. One of the reasons why that boatman resonated with me, I think, and probably the main one, was his being in almost every way and essence like my father, who'd known little of the world beyond working the waves and who found himself already old and hunched at thirty and ancient as the reefs at forty-one. By then, his skin had been baked the yellow tan of summer dirt and weathered coarse as the bark of holly oak, and his eyesight, eroded to ruin from years spent facing into the morning's glare, made do with shadow play and a melancholy awareness of his own end filling the near horizons. In the boatman, I recognised patience, stoicism, a propensity for silence, a certain hardness from a life spent bearing pain, and an innate understanding of the witchery that possesses those who balance their lives on something bottomless and who can accept the floating existence of a life on the water as akin to flying, feeling that same melding sense of the precarious and the euphoric and waiting always for the fall.

Any comparisons with me in all of that have limited themselves largely to surfaces. The difference has to do with courage. In what I'd read, the boatman's only daughter had also died, succumbed to some sweeping fever. That tragedy was for his wife and him a deep one because they'd been blessed to parenthood only late on, nearly twenty years into their marriage. Following a long weekend of mourning, the boatman chose Monday's breaking to slip from the family shack. Carrying the little girl's body wrapped in muslin cloth down to where his home-built sampan sat moored among the rushes, he paddled soundlessly out to sea. And when the land was a thin shadow along the western horizon, and with the crown of the sun coming up as a rust-brown bloodstain ahead of him, he lifted his daughter again, cradled her a moment in his thin arms, then kissed her cold face and her shut eyes and lips, and lowered her body over the side of the boat so that the sea could be her graveyard. His sense was that she'd go into the tide and be lost and absorbed and made a part of everything. And in that way she'd surround him always. Each morning ever after, in rowing out and spreading his nets, he'd think of her and feel her near. His daughter, within the waves, at one with the creatures of the deep. Every drop of the ocean is itself but it's also the ocean.

If I had the courage, I'd follow that lead. My father would have, because when you don't fear death then you fear nothing. Except maybe living. And when you can simply exist, in full acceptance of your lot, then you are immense. Fear is what brings us down and makes small things of us. In all honesty, I don't fear death for myself, but that is nowhere near enough. And I am not the man my father was.

The Chinese believe in reincarnation. That's an idea he'd have liked, if it had ever occurred to him or been put to his mind. He attended Mass because he'd been brought up to do so, the same as everyone else on our island, mumbling the Catholic prayers that we'd all been taught by heart, the strings of words in two languages and stripped of meaning or worth in either one. But anyone who knew him knew that his heart beat for other things. Superstitions, reading signs everywhere, counting particular types of birds at certain times of year, listening out for frogs in the ditches or the wailing of vixens in the night, watching the ruts in the sand, always feeling the air for omens. And, in between, quietly musing about the beautiful details of the world and how they must have come into being, and where certain traits in people came from, and talents. He knew the sea like it had been created with him in mind, knew the tides and currents and where the reefs lay, and when the shoals of mackerel or herring would come and into what waters, as if the hundreds of his line who'd learned the waves inch by inch had educated him through blood and by some unwritten right, gifting him the knowledge.

The surface earth of the graveyard is stiff and dry, but two or three feet down the long build-up of old springtime moisture has held. I sling the pick with a measured frenzy, and the only sounds come from the constant, rhythmic thump of the tool's edge against the dirt and, with every swing, as the ground splits apart in clumps, my own grunting breaths. Michael stands back, watching, then falls in alongside me again with the shovels, and we dig, working in a steady tandem already familiar to us from days spent dealing with things of less importance, and now and then pause to wipe the sweat from our faces. Everything tastes of mud, a dead, mineral grit that fills the lungs, coats tongue and teeth, and holds like an ache to the back of the throat. The sky above us is a dirty colour now, clear but not yet easy with either the swelling light or the loss of darkness, and even though it's still early we are less than halfway done. The funeral is set for eleven but we know that the priest will wait for us, everyone will wait, because waiting is part of it, too, just as much as prayers. Here, on the island, digging is in itself a kind of prayer, and even though weariness eats into us and turns our bones to lead, we won't stop until we've finished the work.

'He won't rot,' someone had said of my father, the night of his wake. A cousin or neighbour, I forget exactly who, but someone known to him in that intimate way of people steeped in one another's lives. And meaning it well, not at all in a crude way but as a kind of deserved immortality. 'Sure at this stage he's more salt than flesh.' Those words had been spoken aloud as mere thought run loose, and others who were in our house that night nodded, and I remember filling my mouth with whiskey straight from a bottle of Jameson that I couldn't recall buying, wanting to be hurt by what had been said, or angry about it or even merely sad, instead of proud, though I'd never have shown it because that's not who we are. Proud that it was my father they were all thinking about, and feeling full of hope that there was truth in what I'd just heard.

I didn't need the confirmation of this moment to know that no such truth existed. But waist-deep in the dirt, stinking of sweat and mud, I get to see that there is nothing left. Even the coffin's brass fittings are gone, either spat out by the rain of eleven years or else sucked down to depths no one would ever reach or ever want to.

I have been thinking about the Chinese boatman as a deflection, because he's a softer, safer thought. My father was not the stuff of stories. He had different trials: the death of a wife early on, and having to see me raised from infancy with little or no help; the two days and a night spent in the water three miles off the island's southern end and clinging to a piece of driftwood after going over-board in a storm; and finally, the stomach cancer that made a husk of him and put him, after a struggle worse

23

than war, into this ground. But his dramas differed only in detail, as they do from the dramas of everybody else, and even though one life was fact and the other a fiction, his soul and that of the boatman's seem to me essentially the same.

Remembering him now hurts bad enough to bleed, yet that is still easier than having to face the facts of Beth, and how little I'd been able to do to help. In the hospital bed, while I stood holding her hand, she looked sad and very small, and even before she closed her eyes for the last time I understood that she and I had miles between us. I failed her, just as I am failing Margaret in not being able to open up, even though my wife needs me now in ways she never has before and even though I want to believe that I'd lay down my life and everything in it for her. The problem is that I've been set adrift, and I've lost sight of who I used to be. On the surface I can be still, and the lack of tears gives me a demeanour of tranquillity that, from a distance, must seem comforting. But my mind is a swept torrent, too packed with the real and the make-believe.

The more I think about that story of the boatman and his daughter, the more I can recognise and appreciate its truth. Because I feel as if I have died a thousand times myself, and that I've known a thousand lives other than this one. Maybe it's just that we're all the same, and perhaps we each get a turn at everything, until we understand. Even if my father is gone, even if there's not a trace of him in the dirt, he's here. Every drop of the ocean is itself but it's also the ocean. And a few hours from now, Beth will be with him. There has to be comfort in that, when it's all we have.

At last, Michael clambers from the hole we've dug, then leans back over the side and extends a hand. I stop digging and look up, wincing against the glare of the heightening day and shielding my eyes with a filthy hand.

'Come on,' he says, his voice brusque with exhaustion. 'That's deep enough. If we go any further, we'll strike oil.'

For several seconds everything is blackness and gold, and it is almost impossible to focus, but then I nod my head, accept the outstretched hand and let myself be hauled back into the world.

# Ruins

We'd spent three late-summer days touring the Beara Peninsula, using the Eccles Hotel in Glengarriff as our base, and even though the third night wrapped itself for a while in a froth of sea mist thick enough to obliterate detail, by six the rain had given way again to a soft grey light. Having kicked loose of the bed sheets, I lay before the opened window, feeling the coolness against my skin. Alongside me Mei slept soundlessly, curled into a loose foetal position, her face inches from mine and combed in shadow. I studied her as the minutes passed, every nerve ending heightened by the sensation of having her so near after so long, until finally she stirred, raised an arm and stretched, her body elongating so that her covering blanket spilt a little away. Her eyes flickered only momentarily open, and just when I'd begun to assume that she had slipped once more into sleep, she murmured something that I didn't understand but which seemed intended as a kind of greeting, and lifted herself in cumbrous fashion across my chest. The morning seeped golden through the gape of the half-curtained window and split the far wall in two, and I tried with everything I had to believe that all of this was real, and that I was here, and alive, and happy. Then her eyes, the colour of a honeycomb's core at that hour, opened wide again and this time fixed on some distant thought, maybe of all the sad mornings that lay ahead for us, after we'd once more taken up our separate fates.

She'd smiled the night before too, in a similarly sad manner, and suggested that there were worse ways to finish, but by then we'd already been over what could be said and when all is already lost it is natural to want to focus only on the contours and colours of the moment. Because of her head's slight incline, most of her hair lay in black webs against the right side of her face, and for a few seconds, without meaning or wanting to, I became a camera, seeing us from somewhere beyond myself and charting everything from that remove. When she raised herself across me and turned a little towards the light I caught tears breaking, sometimes down her face, sometimes clear of her onto the pillow and onto me.

Then, all at once, just as her breath stiffened and the far back of her throat began to find some sound, less even a sound than a vibration, I was within the moment again, and I embraced her tightly. I held her in that way for as long as I could, feeling the bones of her face against mine, and whispering that I loved her, and always would. She looked at me with new intensity then, and as well as I thought I knew her I could also see the scale of her mystery. Her life, even after I'd been allowed inside, was all about walls, and the room she kept for me was exclusive to us but also confined to moments.

'We're together now,' she whispered. 'This is what we have. The world could end tomorrow.'

'My world will end in six days,' I said.

But at this she only sighed. 'No it won't. We'll be sad, but even sad hearts go on beating. Even broken ones.'

The light against the wall waned and the sharpness of the morning was momentarily lost. She stirred when I whispered her name.

'Mei?'

'Hmm.'

'Will you do something for me?'

She smiled. 'What? Again?'

In that moment, in the mixture of light and shade, her face was relaxed, nestled among the chaos of her hair and with the efforts of our exertions still clinging as a gleam across her skin. Her mouth teased with whatever happiness she'd found, but only for a second. Then she looked hard at me.

'What?'

'Marry me,' I said. I reached for her face, combed away loose strands of hair from in front of her eyes, then put the palm of my hand on her cheek. 'You said it yourself. The past is gone and there's only ever now. So, for now, for today, let's marry.'

I waited only a few seconds for an answer that didn't come, then scrambled from the bed. On the writing desk, amid the array of sightseeing leaflets, was a small notepad and hotel pen.

'What are you doing?' she asked, to my back. Laughter and uncertainty set her words to trembling.

'Just an idea,' I said, without turning. It didn't feel quite clean to sit naked on the chair, so I stood there and started to write. Beyond the window and the main road, the sea was a shining veneer around the few thickly foliaged islets, calm as the scudded sky. Small boats hung from their anchors, and a trace of mountains water-coloured the distance along the horizon line. I quickly filled a page and a half, then picked up the pad, read in silence through what I'd scribbled, scratched out and corrected a word or phrase here and there, and finally, with care, tore out the pages.

'The things I want to tell you,' I explained, folding the paper crossways in two and then in two again. 'And that I want you always to know. My vows.'

Her smile straightened but her stare didn't falter. I stood in the middle of the room, thinking that I'd seen her in a few different beds during our broken time together, and I'd never come away unmarked from the melancholy of our aftermaths. Then she ran her hands back through her hair, gathered the blanket, straightened it out over her legs and waist and, without speaking, settled back down on her pillow and turned onto her side, away from me.

It was still early, not yet even seven o'clock, and silent again except for the hush of low waves a hundred yards away, and the occasional music of wrens nesting somewhere close. I'd expected her to drift back into sleep, but when I came out of the bathroom, fifteen or twenty minutes later, refreshed by the shower and drying my hair with a towel, she was sitting up again, with her legs tucked up beneath herself and her head and shoulders over the notepad. She didn't look up, as usual not wanting to admit to having given in, and instead turned to a new page. I stood at the side of the bed and lay a kiss on the exposed side of her neck just beneath her right ear, which caused the world to smell all at once for me of tangerines. Held in place on one thigh, the notepad was flecked in smoothly scratched blue characters. Back when I'd been living in Taipei, I had learned to read a little of these in their printed form, mainly on road and building signs and in the daily newspaper headlines. Handwritten, though, they remained as obscure to me as code.

*

Until the previous February, we'd neither seen nor spoken to one another in twelve years, but there was not a day in all that time that I didn't think about her. Through the first year after we'd parted, and for much of the second, I could hardly function apart from those hours I spent burrowing into whatever story I was trying to make sense of, as much for myself as for any potential reader. I lost weight and then piled it back on in the ugliest and most thickset of ways, drank to be able to sleep, and lived a gulf apart from other people. Some days, even breathing hurt like I'd been set alight. To fill the void I wrote, and whatever came out, fictional or otherwise, revolved around her, around keeping her alive and my agonies fresh. She was my compulsion, and I had nothing else worth saying. Some nights, hours deep inside a new story, I'd lose sight of the screen and be fogged by tears that, once started, came in gouts for long minutes at a time. Afterwards I'd sit there, like a dead tree in a wide field, all stillness and hanging limbs, and cling to the fact that feeling pain was at least still feeling.

If I'd been to war then I'd have written about that. Instead, the fifteen weeks that Mei and I had once shared became my eternity, down to the smallest detail. Leaning into afternoons in that tired Taipei apartment, blinded by the heat and sweating against one another's skin, our bodies each aching to touch, and, once together, singing. Mornings in her uncle's little walk-in restaurant, watching from my seat near the window while she moved among the tables in a short-sleeved cotton dress as glassy-white as seashells, pouring coffee and staring into a space that I tried with all my might to fill. And those evenings sightseeing the city, the bustling, spectacularly strange night markets, the wide-open plaza at Chiang Kai-shek Memorial Hall, where lovers and families congregated to stroll in pairs and packs, and kids watched the soldiers bring down and fold away the flag. Or to the old Longshan Temple, the mood bloated with the stench of open fires and incense, where I cast fate stones while she stood bowing in front of great gold-painted statues of the gods she'd decided at that moment to believe in, just in case they did exist.

I'd known, I think, that a part of who she was had always consisted of some secret or connivance, but her confession, delivered one afternoon when she'd battled through a near-typhoon to spill torrents of herself on my apartment's faded linoleum floor, couldn't have split me open any more decisively with an axe. The second life that she revealed then was, in fact, her real life, and she stood there, beaten wet, talking through tears about the husband at home, a man the past two years crippled and left nearly mute by a deep cerebral haemorrhage. The marriage from the beginning had more to do with security than love, and he being twenty years her senior, long out of shape and not even handsome from a distance, the intimate moments were hard to bear, but until his illness he'd worked hard to make her happy, was always gentle and only ever full of kindness and respect. And for all of those reasons, he was the man she'd accepted in every sense as her other half, for better and for worse.

I hadn't wanted to understand, but did. She was acting out of duty and the need to do what she believed was right. I sat on the side of my bed, unable to even look at her, and after the door was shut behind her there'd been nothing left for me to do but gather the shattered pieces of myself and return home.

In the years that followed, memories were all I had, and I scoured them for insight and lived with them and through them, even on those occasions when I'd find myself pressing the windows of a new romance. As people, we understand when the best has already been and gone, and all that remains to us are shadows. But we have to make the best of things. Mei was always my shadow, the one who loomed across my days and nights even when I was sharing them with someone else, making do with lesser love.

*

We reconnected through the Internet. In the time we'd been apart I'd continued to write, and if fame and wealth had succeeded in eluding me then I was at least still publishing, regular newspaper articles and book reviews, short stories at a slow but consistent pace for middling to decent literary magazines and journals, mostly in the States where there was still a fairly buoyant market for the type and length of stuff I tended to produce, and a novel or new collection every two or three years. I was filling days and passing time, and getting by as best I could.

'You probably won't remember me,' she'd written, in an email that almost stopped my heart and which I read repeatedly over the next several hours, unable to quite believe what I was seeing. 'But you and I were close friends once, in Taipei. The best friend I ever had. I think of you often, and it pleases me to see that you still write books, and I hope you are well, and happy.'

'Of course I remember you,' I wrote back, after a day spent shaping my reply, having edited anger down to bitterness and then to nearly unbearable truth, deciding that honesty could cost me nothing more than I'd already lost. 'I remember every inch of you, and my heart is broken still because of it. But even though there were nights when thinking of all I'd lost made me want to die, I know that I'm so much better for having known you.'

'I miss you, too,' she replied, within minutes. 'Night and day, I miss you, too.' And on the next line: 'Love, always.' Unsigned, but a statement, as I chose to read it, of intent as well as fact.

Weeks of messages and grabbed calls followed then, making craters of the time in between, stripping my life once again of everything but us. I clung to my email account and barely slept, not wanting to live even a second in blindness to one of her responses. The eight hours of time difference didn't matter because my body clock set itself as if I'd been waiting always for this chance, and within a couple of days, my hands shaking and my breath feeling like rocks in my throat, I was dialling the number she'd given me. 'Wéi,' she'd say, on answering the phone, *yes* as both an acknowledgement and a permission, her voice coming vague and distant and exactly as it had always sounded, even when she was against me, frail and full of air but also laced with all the things that didn't belong in words. I took care not to push for details, and most of my questions hung unasked, afraid of breaking whatever spell we'd forged. She read my book every night, she said, the book I'd written before arriving in Taipei. My first, proud as I was of it, was a collection of short stories so separate from me by now, so belonging to my life before this life, that it hardly felt like mine at all any more. I'd left a copy with her, scrawling something either ridiculously formal or stupidly its opposite into the title page, *kind regards*, or *happy reading*; innocuous and anaemic words, perhaps, when there'd been such an opportunity to reveal myself, but a compromise that allowed her to justify my place on her bookshelf, or at her bedside. And shyly, it seemed to me, as if she were confessing to some sinful act, she admitted that not even one night had passed since my leaving without her picking up those stories and poring over a page or even just a few lines. She still read English slowly and badly but, after twelve years, had come to know their contents nearly by heart. I told her that I'd written other books since then, novels as well as collections, and some were better than others but all were better than that first one because they'd all, in their different ways, been shaped by her. But the book she had was good enough, she said, because it had allowed her to keep my voice in her head through all that time. And in her favourite stories, the saddest ones, every sentence I'd written sounded exactly like me. Hearing this made me happy, knowing that I'd been with her as much and as continuously as she'd been with me, but it also made me sad, because the years we'd lost, the time we'd wasted on loneliness, felt magnified.

Sometimes I'd put down the phone and start typing, and the words that came were like howls, full of all the things I'd wanted to say to her but couldn't because the distance between us was still immense and the renewed link too tenuous. Such as how foolish I'd been, and how weak, to have let her indulge in doing the right thing at the cost of what we had going. Such as how, if I'd been any sort of man at all, I'd have shaken her into seeing sense, I'd have grabbed her and held on, and dragged her with me when I ran, damning the consequences, damning all voices of conscience and duty. We'd lost twelve years because she had put her crippled, brain-damaged husband's greater needs ahead of her own happiness and mine too, and even though what we kept, each in our own tragic way, was still a love of sorts, it had been stretched too wide and punished too much with silence and lack of touch. Regret, we'd both come to realise, was a far greater burden to bear than guilt. Guilt hadn't the permanence of regret, and could be kissed and laughed away. We'd have found healing through moments of simple ease: a walk in the woods or along the seashore, holding hands, speaking in murmured smiles and settling for the gentle reassurances of one another's touch. That was the opportunity we'd had and not taken, and instead we came to understand the hard way that you indulge in guilt but live with regret, and it turns the taste of everything and makes you lonesome day and night.

\*

By nine, we'd breakfasted and were on the road back to Cork. But there was no hurry.

Kealkill, a picturesque village tucked into the foot of a steep hillside roughly halfway between Bantry and the old monastic settlement of Gougane Barra, was quiet even for a Sunday, a pristine cluster of homes, shops and pubs. The morning felt ripe with promise, and a skin of translucent cloud draped the distance ahead, skirting the climbing sun. All along the roadside, flaming blooms of lupin, sea aster, bindweed and dog rose gave the morning a rare brilliance.

The stone circle was signposted, and the car took the hill slowly, straining in places against the incline. We picked our steps along the high part of the first field, keeping to where the earth had been sculpted into ruts by tractor wheels and blanched from weeks of wind and dry weather. Then, after coming through a gap in the ditch, the stones rose up ahead of us: two of them, side by side, the smaller of the pair taller than the height of a man with his arms raised, the larger probably half that height again; and to their left, as we cleared a brow in the land, five flat-faced stones of varying size laid out with meticulous care in a snug ten-foot circle.

On the drive out, Mei had listened while I talked of the place's importance to our earliest people and the mystical quality of the circles in marking out sacred locations for the ancients, and she watched the road from the passenger seat and made small sounds of understanding while sunlight jabbed between the branches of the roadside trees and lit her face in staccato bolts. But nothing I'd said came close to the feeling of actually standing here, catching from those great schist slabs that strange sense of a time out of time, the kind of unyielding permanence that makes death seem superficial. There was such a holiness about this place, one that tuned itself to deepest, oldest magic, and I could see its effect on Mei, in the slow way she moved and the distance in her eyes when she rested her hands on one of the stones; and I could feel it in myself.

We walked among the stones, trying to concentrate on the thrum of the earth alive beneath us, and took turns at feeling small in a few photographs, pressing ourselves one at a time in against the taller of the monoliths and laughing for the camera. And within the circle, time stopped. The green hills ahead of us wore layers of themselves into the distance, and Bantry Bay lay off to the west of us, a cobalt spread folded in between the slants of land and the huge deepening sky.

All playfulness ceased, and I took her in my arms. As we came together I felt her whisper something, some reflex thought shaped in her own language, but it broke in two against my mouth, went unfinished and was lost. Later, when I mentioned it, wanting to know what it was that she'd started to say and what it meant, she either didn't understand what I was asking or had no recollection of having spoken at all. Even though it probably wasn't anything important, merely an expression of the view's beauty or the idyll of the moment, for some reason losing those words bothered me and left me with a feeling of disquiet. But in the circle, then, with her that close, the two of us breathing and tasting of one another, words hardly mattered. When we drew apart, she smiled and lowered her eyes, and I kept my arms around her and told her what I wanted.

'This is a special place,' I said, in that instant believing it. 'Time has no meaning here.'

I kicked off my shoes and socks and rolled the legs of my jeans up over my calves. After a few seconds she followed my lead, standing awkwardly first on one foot and then the other, leaning against me. Beneath us the long grass was cool and soft, but the earth had its own warmth. Her feet were white and sweetly fleshy, and her toes clenched at first but then stretched open and I could see pleasure in her face at the recollection of this feeling from childhood days when summers were often spent barefoot.

Our period of separation had altered details of her, tightened the corners of her mouth, maybe took a little of the sheen from the skin beneath her eyes. But she was still the beauty she'd always been. My grandmother used to say that absence makes the heart grow fonder, and I suppose in my case at least, having thought of nobody else since our parting, even when there'd been occasionally others to think about, and having filtered every word of everything I'd written over the past twelve years through the memory of her, that had proven true.

'Okay,' she whispered, while I dug in my pocket for the folded sheets of paper. I could feel the tremble in her voice. 'I'll marry you. I'll play. And we'll be happy, for the time we have left. Only, don't ask for more. And don't think about forever.'

'Up here,' I said, trying to smile, 'now is forever.'

But she shook her head. Tears were in her eyes and trying not to fall.

'Please, Billy. I won't leave him. You asked that of me before, and my answer is the same. What we want doesn't matter.'

I thought I'd feel differently, and that something would have altered in our relationship. Sweet as it was, though, our moment proved simply of itself, another of the best details stamped into our time together but a gesture and, for all that, a performance, and afterwards the world continued to turn in its usual way, dragging us slowly yet again apart.

In the circle, I read aloud the vows I'd written and my life has never known moments of greater intimacy. While I was speaking, and then while she was, nothing existed outside of that ten-foot circle. The skin of her hand was hot from my touch and full of pulse, and she hung on every word I recited and mouthed my own phrases back at me, the most vital ones, forging a soundless chain of them in some desperate attempt at permanence. Making sculptures of them.

When it was her turn to speak, she became embarrassed. A smile whetting her mouth, she raised her pages and began, with some hesitation, to read in very slow

Chinese. Once I stopped expecting a translation I relaxed so completely to the cadence of her voice, the tone rippling between highs and flats, that I was able to catch the ending, when it came, as forced and cut short, a hesitation that widened into greater silence, and though I didn't challenge her on it I knew that she'd settled things in too broken a way and that some important sentiment had gone unsaid. She watched me, the sheets of paper still in one hand, folded back along their lines into a small rectangle, and it took me a second to be able to breathe again, and to smile, and, finally, to open my arms for her.

'I wonder,' I said, speaking against the skin below her ear, 'if we're the first people to ever marry within this circle. But who knows, maybe this is actually what it was for.'

And maybe to preserve the moment, or just to silence me, she moved in my arms and found my mouth, and I closed my eyes and told myself that this at least was something new, not for the world but for us, our first coming together as husband and wife, and a sense of life coursed through me and I hoped through her, too, the same river flow, bringing thoughts and taking them back, awakening our histories and fusing them together, even when they couldn't properly fit. But while nothing stops time quite like a kiss, and nothing makes so much of a moment, no kiss lasts forever.

I reached for the sheets of paper that she held crumpled in her fist, attempted to smooth them out and examine them in search of revelation, then asked that she tell me what she'd written, what the words meant.

But she just smiled. 'Keep them if you want,' she said, turning from me, opening herself again to the view. 'You know they talk about love. But don't ask for more. Let the rest be mystery.'

*

In the days following, knowing the value of what I had and was about to lose, I lived as much as possible in the moment. Waking early to watch Mei sleep, filling myself with details of her; brushing our teeth together at the bathroom sink, watching one another in the mirror; soaping her back and feeling the soft and hard places while she sat in the bath with her knees pulled up against her breasts and her arms embracing her shins. There was so much to be said but silence was just easier, and our stares held for long moments, across rooms and close up, already filling up with the loneliness that lay ahead.

On the morning of her flight, I woke to an empty bed. It was still dark, which would have put the time at somewhere between probably four and five, and at first I lay there, feeling bereft. I listened for the sound of her, but the radio in the corner of the room was playing low, a rope of old songs, the words and melodies of which kept her hidden. Early Tom Waits; Cohen's 'Suzanne'; Marianne Faithfull singing 'Ruby Tuesday'. Music made with the smallest hours in mind. Outside my window, rhapsodies of gale pulled at the jagged top of a young roadside hawthorn, and even though the glass kept the sound at bay, the wind's ferocity set the few scattered stars to shimmering and made shreds of the night.

Even without Mei in the room, her presence blocked out the space the way sand fills an hourglass, turning everything slow. That's how I wanted it to be, and that at least was what I'd have, but I knew from before, from having already lost her once, such ghosts tormented as much as consoled. We'd taken an important step in reconnecting and had sworn we wouldn't let that flag, so that it would be different this time, better even if still a long way from ideal, but keeping our promise meant condemning ourselves to a famished life, to the scraps that could nourish only the most fragile of hearts. In taking from a kind word and a smile far more than such gestures could ever truly give, we were committing to a delusion, but survival for most people owed an immense debt to lies, because lies were what kept us all still swinging long after the fighting was done.

When the time passed and she didn't return, I got up and went to find her. She was in the living room, sitting on a hard chair beside the glass door that gave out onto my balcony, and so tucked into the shadow that at first I didn't even see her. A nearby street light sprayed its thin sheen across the glass and part of the floor.

'Mei,' I whispered, a little intimidated by the dark. 'What are you doing up? Come back to bed. We only have a few more hours.'

I came to the brink of the light but held back for just a moment because I was naked and could have been seen from the road or from other windows. She had her hair down around her shoulders in jet cascades and was wearing a long sleeveless nightgown, pink and mottled with tiny flowers, that seemed to absorb rather than deflect the darkness.

'I'm cold,' she said, turning away from me again, to the balcony laden with baskets of geraniums and chamomile daisies, petunias, morning glory and swathes of lobelia, and to the road and facing houses. The flesh of her upper arm was cool and soft, pliable to the pressure of my touch but already numbing itself against me. I felt her sigh, and then she stood and let me lead her back to bed. Beneath the covers we held one another tight and didn't speak, and at some point, as dawn began to break unseen except as a pink reflection in the glass of the windows opposite, I helped her peel off her nightgown and we made love one more time, quietly except for whimpers that sounded like squeals of pain but weren't, as she reached her high place and as I climbed hurriedly towards mine.

At the airport I stood with her in line to clear security, holding her hand and whispering to her how much I'd miss her until we could see each other again and how we had to promise to email every day and to call one another at least twice a week. She looked serious and sad, and I knew that she was fighting to keep herself together, and in her face I saw an exact reflection of the way I felt. It was in my mouth to ask if she might change her mind, if she'd throw aside her morals and stay with me. She'd already given up so much for a situation that could only ever worsen, and with me there was at least a chance at happiness. But she'd heard these thoughts from me too many times. When it was her turn to pass through security, we kissed goodbye. The press of her mouth was familiar and gently firm, and tears spilt down her cheeks and onto mine, tears that'd come in floods for hours more, on the plane, with her face turned in a vain attempt at privacy to the small window, looking out on a scarred tundra of rain cloud.

I watched until she slipped away and out of sight, and the void was exactly as I remembered. I sat for a while with a paper cup of coffee in one of the airport cafes, and it was easier to pass the time there than at home, because the apartment would seem so hollow after her and at least in the airport it was possible to feel that she was still close by. But an hour later, after the departures screen listed her flight as having left, I left too. I was limp inside, and home proved as bare and haunted as I'd feared, the silence a kind of roar around me. Trying to busy myself, I cooked something, chopping and stir-frying chicken, a sliced green pepper and green beans, favouring this because it kept me at the stove. Later, once night had taken hold, I switched on the computer and wrote a little, not concentrating, just letting it flow, the way I always did when things turned particularly difficult. Because this, as anyone who has ever had their heart broken by love knows, is how it has to be. The tide comes in and then recedes, and we stand and wait for it to come again. So much of life is waiting, but even ruined as we are, waiting at least makes room for dreams.

# Beginish

They'd worked hard all winter, Isabelle putting in early shifts at the bakery and wiping down tables three evenings a week at a small vegetarian restaurant, Thomas taking advantage of the current financial boom to pick up work on one or another of the building sites strewn across the city: six weeks here, a couple of months there, the best of the jobs cash in hand for the long hours of hauling blocks and barrows of rubble. Life went on hold as, every night and tired to their bones, they slumped down together on their old sofa, and sometimes it took an hour of Isabelle's gentle nagging before Thomas could rouse himself enough to take a shower, even though he reeked of sweat and his face was scorched from a day spent shovelling cement and mixing concrete. When they finally crawled into bed, too weary to concentrate on whatever was flashing across the television screen, sleep came almost instantly for him, but she usually resisted the pull, preferring to savour the late torpor, and she'd lie there on her side of their narrow mattress, tucked in against the wall and snug beneath the covers, with an arm draped across his chest trying to feel and measure his heartbeat and his dreams. Everything about him tasted always now of dust, even after he'd washed, and his skin had a parched, woody coarseness. The thin, slightly stooped boy that she'd first met some four years earlier was gone; manual labour had lengthened his six-foot frame and turned him broad across the shoulders. And she fell harder for him with every passing day. When he moved against her or when, as often still happened, especially on weekends, they'd wake ahead of the alarm clock and he'd lift himself up so that she could slip beneath him, his body had an assured heft.

He was twenty-seven, she'd not long turned twenty-three, and they had married the previous July, in a simple registry office ceremony witnessed by his father and brother, two of her cousins, and a few friends. The marriage was something he'd pushed for, despite her continual insistence that their love needed no such certifying, and she'd only given in when, having tried everything else, he began shaping the argument in legal terms. One Sunday morning, during those languid minutes after making love, and with the darkness of the small hours still thick as blankets around them, she'd lain with her head against his chest and her fingers teasing half a dozen inches of the skin around his navel, and whispered in happy sighs of them being entirely one, heart and soul, body and mind. 'Yeah,' he'd answered, kissing the top of her head. 'That's true for today. But imagine if something happens. Either to me or to you. From that moment on, someone else will own the other half of us. When it comes to next of kin, the law is strict about such things.'

Home – a rented, middle-floor bedsit of a three-storey house in Dillon's Cross – wasn't much, but didn't need to be. Possessions didn't matter; what they desired most was freedom, and to be free together. For now, and to open up that future for themselves, all they needed was a place to live, food to eat, and a bed to share. The rent on the bedsit was low, which allowed them to put aside a considerable portion of their earnings – as much as three or even four hundred, some weeks, if Thomas caught some overtime – and its location, little more than a fifteen-minute walk down the steep northside to the city centre, made it ideal for getting to and from work.

*

Through the winter, all their talk had been of escape. With rain or hail scudding the amber-lit glass, they read intrepid travelogues and picked through the clammy, full-colour, library-copy pages of *National Geographic* on the wonders of the South Pacific. The Marquesas, Tuvalu, Pitcairn, the Marshall Islands; places exotic in both name and fact that barely freckled atlas maps. Such fantasies suited grey days and long nights but gradually, as spring approached, their sights began to shift in more realistic directions.

'I've been thinking,' Isabelle said, one morning in late March. She was sitting on the bed, naked except for one of Thomas's old oversized T-shirts, and with a mug of green tea in one hand and a triangle of buttered toast held delicately in the other. 'As great as Polynesia sounds, we have islands here at home, too. And what do we care, really, when all is said and done, about the weather? I mean, neither one of us can even swim.'

49

Thomas stood across the room, at the toaster, in just his boxer shorts, waiting for two more slices of bread to brown. The radio had just dispensed with the 6 a.m. news and was full of Talking Heads, 'Once in a Lifetime', and wind from the west flayed the glass in occasional gusts, whistling whenever it caught a split in the window's old, rotting frame. Sleep was still on him, and his eyes kept sticking to corners. But when her words filtered through, he looked up.

'You're right,' he said, after several seconds of consideration, his voice hushed with something like wonder. 'All we're after, really, is somewhere big enough for the two of us, a place where we can be away from everything and everyone. That's it, isn't it? I don't mean to own, and we're not even talking about forever, but just to try for a few weeks. A month, maybe. A bit of ground, the sea and sky. And us. Our very own Eden.'

'Do you think we can, though?' Isabelle chewed at one corner of her toast. 'I mean, is it even allowed? We'd probably need all kinds of permission. It sounds like way too much fun. There's bound to be some law against it.'

But a seed was set, and in the weeks that followed, the idea turned into an obsession, until they thought of almost nothing else. Their reading habits changed. He studied maps and researched tides and fishing techniques, the most efficient ways to light campfires, and how to build safe and solid shelter in the wild. She combed library books and documentary channels for tips on living off the land, what could be eaten in terms of berries and leaves, and what could not. The trick, they both gradually decided, was to start gently, to give themselves a taste of it, keeping the getaway to just a month at first and hauling a small but sufficient supply of backup rations. And if all went well, Thomas said, they could consider it a trial run and start thinking about making it a whole new way of life.

'Just the essentials. Tins of food, beans, fish, maybe some cured meat. In case of emergency.'

'Don't forget water,' she added. 'Because it'd be just our luck to walk into a heatwave.'

'Funny.'

'Seriously, though. I can hardly believe how excited I am about this. It'll be the honeymoon we never had.'

He looked at her, and smirked. 'I hadn't thought of that.'

'That's because I'm the brains of this outfit.'

'True enough,' he said, with a shake of his head. 'But maybe that's where we've been going wrong.'

*

Following a careful surveying of the coastline, both in books and on the Internet, they fixed on the Blaskets as their most viable option. The tight cluster of islands just a few miles off one of Kerry's more remote corners had been evacuated back in the 1950s, when it was felt that the safety of the inhabitants could no longer be assured, and though they'd remained uninhabited, in recent years a solid tourist industry had blossomed around them. During the long season that thrived between March and October, throngs of middle-aged, raincoat-clad Americans and Europeans arrived at the state-of-the-art visitors' centre perched on the final few yards of the Dingle Peninsula to wander among the various exhibitions and audio-visual demonstrations of long-ago island life before shuffling as a pack down to Dún Chaoin harbour and boarding the ferry for an excursion across to the main island. There, accompanied by one or another of the young students claiming a blood connection with the place in order to earn some summer cash, they picked through the remnants of the near and ancient past, grinning all the while with delight at their guide's accent and hanging on every sing-song syllable of the stories being spun: a hard twist of history and fantasia, bookish facts on the earliest settlements as well as more colourful tales, either handed down or simply fabricated, of shipwrecks, piracy and perfect storms, of the ravaging Famine days and the final heartbreaking government-enforced exodus.

About halfway between the Great Island and the mainland at Dunmore Head, probably not even a mile from shore, Thomas and Isabelle found what they'd been seeking. Elevated to some fifty feet or so above the tide and, at thirty relatively flat acres, little more than a good-sized farm, Beginish was ground abandoned to weather and wildlife, providing a safe haven for grey seals and summering Arctic terns. It seemed ideal; small, safe, private, with the crumbling stumps of a single cottage and shed the only indication that people had ever inhabited the place at all, and yet within easy enough reach of civilisation, should a sudden need arise.

By May, after fully committing to the decision, they had begun attending to practical details. Rather than having to waste a month's rent, they gave notice on the bedsit, agreeing to move out on the last day of July. Work, for Thomas, on a multi-storey car park on Union Quay, was due to finish in the middle of that month, which worked out nicely; and arranging time off proved no great obstacle for Isabelle, either, especially once she explained that this was to be their first getaway as husband and wife, something she'd been yearning for, without really believing they'd ever be able to afford it, since the day of their wedding. On hearing this, the bakery allowed her two weeks' paid holidays, and a fortnight more unpaid, while the restaurant, which employed her on nothing more than a casual basis anyway, simply put her job on hold, ready and waiting to be taken up again on her return. Furthermore, her friend Liz, who worked with her at the bakery, had a spare bedroom and insisted on stowing their meagre belongings: some clothes, shoes, a few books, a small photo album and a laptop computer, all of which fitted with ease into two medium-sized cardboard boxes.

The final piece of their plan clicked into place when a short online search turned up a man in Dingle who agreed to sell them a small rowboat on the condition, put forward by Isabelle, that he'd buy it back from them within six weeks for half the twelve hundred that he was asking. And for an extra fifty, he was even willing to haul it to their chosen collection point. Isabelle spoke with him on the phone and told him of their intentions, her enthusiasm making a torrent of her words, and he listened through it all, gurgling what sounded like laughter into the silences between her sentences, either thinking her a touch mad or else assuming that the entire scheme was a cover for some hare-brained smuggling racket. But with the money already on his mind he didn't much care what they were about. 'Your man can row the distance easily enough,' was all he said, his broad accent making a soft hush of his S's. 'It's not that far if he just goes nice and steady. Take a bit of free advice, and try to catch a high tide, if you can. But don't start out if the water's any way rough. She's a grand little boat, solid out, and she probably wouldn't roll in anything less than a storm, but you don't want to be taking risks.'

*

On the first day of August, a Thursday just ahead of the holiday weekend, they stood each with an arm around the other's back on the almost deserted beach at Dunmore Head and looked out over the water at the small green platform of land that they'd be calling home for the next few weeks. They were tired and happy, having spent most of the night awake, packing rucksacks with sleeping bags, a couple of scant changes of clothes, raincoats and a warm jacket each, as well as their various supplies of knives, spoons, a sewing kit, a small hatchet, matches, tinned and vacuum-packed food, and two bottles of whiskey that they'd bought as potential defence against the rawness of the nights to come and which, Isabelle knew, Thomas would delight in rationing with an almost ritualistic fervour. All the way here, through a long, stifling day of travelling, by bus to Dingle, where they stocked up on fifteen two-litre bottles of water in one of the supermarkets, and then the last twenty miles or so by taxi, their minds were overrun with thoughts of what lay ahead. But it was only now, standing here on the sand with the sea and the island actually in sight, that the whole adventure felt truly, finally real.

The boat was waiting down near a small outcropping of reef. The seller, Paudie Joe, in a tobacco-coloured suit and a whitish shirt with three-quarters of its buttons undone and a brown homburg screwed onto his head at a hard tilt, was sitting on the bow, reading a brutally dishevelled newspaper. He looked up only when they approached, shook hands with them both and, with a slight nod of his head, folded away Isabelle's cash in an inside jacket pocket.

'You found the place, so,' he said, after wiping his face and the back of his neck with an oily handkerchief. 'Well, ye've a grand day for it, anyway.'

The early afternoon had finally caught the lightest breeze, and the water ahead of them was a bed of light: pale blue in the distance beneath an only slightly deeper and immaculately unblemished sky but in close a shimmering white fire so brilliant that it branded echoes of itself into their vision.

Paudie Joe helped drag the boat down the few yards of beach, and held it steady on the water's edge while Thomas gathered their belongings and lifted Isabelle aboard.

'Right, I'd say you're about set, so.' He straightened up, and shook hands with them both again. 'This weather, there won't be any great pull, but if you're new to the water you'll still likely be surprised at how much there is. Just take it handy. Even at a crawl you'd cross there in fifteen, twenty minutes. And ye look like ye have all the gear. I suppose there's no point in me asking if ye know what ye're doing.'

From her place in the boat, Isabelle smiled. 'None at all,' she said, and after a second he smiled too, and tossed his head and shoulders in a quick shrug.

'Well, take care, so. And I'll see ye in a few weeks' time, please God.'

For a minute or two, until they'd settled themselves properly, they let the boat drift. Even in the first few feet of water, and with the sea as tranquil as it could ever be, their balance felt compromised. The waves this close to the beach were low but quick ahead of breaking, and the task they'd set themselves seemed suddenly immense. Thomas sat just forward of the boat's centre, facing the strand, and settled the oars into their locks but didn't yet begin to pull. His hand shifted and re-gripped the handles, seeking comfort and stability. Isabelle, perched in the stern barely an arm's reach away, huddled forward with her elbows on her knees, and had to take her balance from him. She wasn't smiling now, and the skin at the corners of her mouth held little brackets.

To put her at ease, he grinned. 'Fifteen or twenty minutes, the man said. What does he think I am? Some kind of pirate? A mile's a hell of a distance for the likes of me.'

'He's the pirate, I'd say.' She considered the boat with an exaggerated scepticism.

'Well, there are a couple of life jackets, if we need them.'

But the fun of the words relaxed her, and after Thomas had hauled them a hundred yards out from the beach, she shifted her position, leaned back and stretched out her legs so that her feet settled between his. She was barefoot, dressed in denims cut off in a rough fringe high up along her thighs, and her legs were long, the flesh milky after the long winter. He had an urge to reach out for her, to drop the oars and run his hands up over her, and when he met her eyes again he saw by the way she was looking at him that she had read his mind.

'Sorry,' he said. 'I lost my bearings for a second.'

'They're not lost,' she said, lifting a foot up along the inside of his bare calf and arching it to rest against his knee. 'I know exactly where they are. And where they need to stay, at least until we reach land.'

At the halfway point, he stopped rowing. The shoreline had become a golden stripe of sand, back among the darker ridges of the headland. Out this far, the breeze was soft and deceptive, masking the afternoon's fire, and the exertion of rowing had coated his arms and face in sweat. The muscles across his shoulders and back felt good in their flexing, but he and Isabelle had made it almost to within touching distance of their destination now and there was no need to hurry. He raised the oars and, one-handed, awkwardly, slipped out of his T-shirt. Isabelle watched, then followed suit. Then, after just the briefest hesitation, she pulled the string of her bikini top, too.

'Pretty nice view from out here,' he murmured, with a little teasing cough inside the words.

The sea was a constant hush, splashing in slops where it caught the sides of the boat. Isabelle leaned back onto her elbows, in a way that flattened her small breasts to her chest, and closed her eyes. The rods of her ribcage latticed her skin, and shallow but obvious trenches emphasised her collarbones, but she'd never looked more relaxed or more beautiful. Out here, with the beach so far away, they might have been the last two people left on Earth.

'I wish this could last forever,' she sighed, without opening her eyes. 'Isn't it just perfect?'

He sat watching her, watching how her stomach flattened and hollowed to the unhurried tide of her breathing, and thinking about something he'd once read or been told, which was that everybody had to decide for themselves what happiness looked like. Nobody had ever lit him up like she could. She wore her hair, that woody shade of hazel which in some clouded light seemed to shine almost grey and in others possessed a nearly greenish tint, cut up in a short, dense pageboy style that lent small magnificence to the sculpture of her face, the strong cheekbones and even the gentle overbite, and she stretched out in pencil lines against the boat's old wood, her upper body's weight set back on her elbows causing her narrow shoulders to jut. There'd be nothing without her, he decided, at least nothing worth knowing.

And just then, for barely an instant, something shifted inside the day, the slightest waning, the insinuation of a shadow. For that half a heartbeat, the water lost the apex sharpness of its glimmer and turned instead steely, and the heat within the day grew overwhelming. Everything was quickly right again and as before, but even so, he set the paddles of the oars back in the water.

'Hold off on that thought,' he said, trying to put a smile into the words, but not fully feeling it. 'Let's wait until we have solid ground beneath us before you go saying things like that. We can wait a few more minutes for perfection.'

And feeling once more for the rhythm, he began to drag at the oars again as, out ahead of him, and behind her, the land lay in a smudged line above the water and looked less and less like a place they'd ever known.

The easiest place to land on Beginish was a snug strip of beach on the far side of the island, which meant a further ten or fifteen minutes of rowing. In close to the rocks, the current had a stronger and less predictable grasp, and once they rounded the jut of reef and were faced, away to the west, with nothing but open sea, the pull on the boat became increasingly significant. From all he'd read on the subject, Thomas had expected as much, and so he'd believed himself prepared, but now an anxiety settled into him and wouldn't let go. Isabelle sensed his tension too and she straightened up from her slouch, fixed her stare on the island's stony barricades and studied the rippling water for some treacherous flash of reef. All along this side of Beginish, the water broke in small white explosions against the rocks, shredding itself open and apart against the island, and then the stripe of strand rose into view and Isabelle gave a little gasp of relief and lurched forward, straining to focus on something out past her husband's left shoulder. 'I can see it,' she said, her voice gleeful, and she let her hand settle in a loose grip around his right wrist. 'A gorgeous white piece of beach. We're here, Tom. We're almost home.'

They dragged the boat high up onto the sand and Thomas lashed its lead rope to one of the rocky outcroppings. Care in all things, he'd read, even though August was just breaking and it seemed an unnecessary precaution. The beach was a beautiful spot, the very definition of 'private', a discreet horseshoe cove sheltered all along its back side by a towering ridge and with unbroken views clear to the western horizon. The water, even just a few yards out, was very deep, with currents and rip tides that made swimming a risk, but the sand was clean and fine and, on days like this one, it seemed nothing short of paradise. He gazed out at the water and was tempted, just for a minute, to simply throw himself down and sleep, because the fatigue which stress and the need for exertion had held in check all morning now closed in around him.

'There's a path,' Isabelle said, coming to him at an easy jog. 'I didn't think there was at first, but you can definitely make it out if you look closely.'

Thomas considered the sweep of footprints that rumpled the sand off towards the nearer, northern end of the beach, but when no path was immediately obvious he started away in that direction. Isabelle remained by the boat, then changed her mind and skipped after him.

'See,' she said, pointing out where the vaguest suggestion of a track wound its way up through a smothering of briar to the ground above.

'Christ, Izzy,' he said, 'we'll be torn to rags. If there even is a path there, I doubt it's been used in decades.'

'Well, from what I can see, it's either this or trying to climb that wall of rock. But if you can see another way, I'd love to hear about it.'

He looked at her. 'Did I at least think to pack some pairs of jeans?'

'I hope so,' she said, stripping out of her shorts down to the most indiscreet of bikini bottoms and stretching herself out on the sand. 'For the sake of those lovely legs.'

After a few seconds spent glaring at her and being wilfully ignored, he sighed theatrically and began to rummage through his belongings, burrowing to the bottom of his rucksack for the hatchet, then pulling on his denims and, after the briefest hesitation, his second pair.

Even though there was evidence up close of a trail beneath the brush, the first few paces into the slope met with considerable obstruction, by clawing fronds of briar woven into a thick mesh across the mouth of the path. The hatchet proved inefficient, and useless against anything that hadn't set solid, so Thomas's best option was to simply trample his way through. It wasn't easy either, but it worked, and within an hour he'd flattened a basic path to the top fields. He stood on the higher ground then, surveying the acreage in a lazy sweep, the land one long, gently undulating roll of grass apart from where the rocks poked through. Off to his right stood the skull-and-bone leftovers of the island's single dwelling, a ruin of what had once, and probably for a century or even two, been a shepherd's cottage. First glance suggested it to be nothing but rubble, but the gable end remained standing, putting a strong back to any wind that might swing in from the west. That wall, he decided, would serve as their back, too, in supporting their shelter, and he let his mind fill up with thoughts of how good an idea all of this was, how idyllic the time they'd spend here would be. There were no sounds apart from the frothy coughing of the waves breaking against the reefs back along the island's high end and the occasional call of a passing gannet or petrel.

*

Towards the end of their first week the weather started to turn. Isabelle was again down on the beach – enjoying the sun, as she did for a couple of hours during the hottest stretch of most afternoons – when she felt the shift: something subtle about the glow of the light, and a guttering to the slightest breeze that plucked small peaks into the ocean's surface. She wasn't afraid. Instead of hurrying back to their shelter, she stood for a long time just where the tide rolled up onto the sand, feeling the electricity in the day and how it seemed to move against her in walls, not wind yet, not exactly that, but a definite shift in atmosphere. She knew without ever having seen this before that the sea was set to roughen and that by the following morning, or maybe even the arrival of night, the waves would be rolling in high. When eventually she climbed the path she saw Thomas over on the island's highest point, also looking westward. He'd felt the difference, too, he said, when she came to stand beside him, and was trying to read the signs, to make out what mattered and what didn't, because even though whatever was happening hardly bothered the day in a visible sense, and even though the sky remained clear, at least for now, there were more gulls than usual down among the rocks, and out in the water vague, crawling shadow lines seemed to stripe the distance, as if something huge was rising from the depths.

Dusk was already upon them by the time they returned to their camp to prepare supper. Until then the tent had gone largely unused except as a place of storage because, most nights, they'd chosen to sleep outside, finding comfort against one another in a large shared sleeping bag and lying awake in one another's arms deep into the smallest hours, listening to the sound of the waves lapping at the island's fringes and gazing up at the stars sprayed with such density across the sky. Thomas checked the tent's ropes and stakes, and further secured any that had begun to slacken, then set about building a fire, using dried kelp and dead grass to catch the flame and stoking it in sparing fashion with a few small pieces of the drift-wood that he'd salvaged from the rocks their third or fourth day here. Out of habit, he lit the fire behind the stone stumps at the far end of the ruined cottage, so that it would be mostly shielded from both the mainland and the other islands.

Once the flames took hold, Isabelle set down a pot with water to boil for coffee, and a small pan, into which she laid a chunk of butter and four thickly cut strips of bacon. While the bacon was frying, she emptied a tin of baked beans into the pan, and readied two plates.

They ate without hurry, sitting cross-legged on the grass, the cast of the fire brightening their faces.

'It's a long time since I remember food tasting this good,' Thomas said, using the pad of his thumb to wipe his plate clean of tomato sauce.

'Bacon and beans.' She smiled. 'Nectar of the gods. I just wish we had a slice of bread and butter to go with it.'

'We better make the most of this, though, because if the weather turns bad on us this'll likely be the last hot food we have for a while. Keeping a fire lit is tough enough at the best of times, but factor in the wind and rain and you can just about forget it.'

Isabelle looked up, thinking that it was difficult to imagine a more beautiful night. The sky was still clear, apart from a small wall of horizon cloud shining with the blood-orange stains left behind by the sinking sun. Away in the opposite direction, the empty blueness had already deepened enough for the first stars to have pressed into view. 'We might be spared the rain,' she said. 'We might be lucky.'

They weren't. That night, at Thomas's insistence, they slept in the tent, and it was strange at first to be so confined after the recent nights of freedom, but when Isabelle woke shortly before dawn to the torrential drum-beating of the rain against the pitched roof and canvas walls, her first thought was one of immense relief for this shelter, however limited. She crawled from the sleeping bag without disturbing Thomas, and undid a little of the door flap's upper binding. The island was awash, the rain so smothering that no morsel of detail survived.

Soon after, Thomas woke. He sat up and listened.

'How bad is it?'

'Bad,' she said. 'You'd have to swim to get anywhere in that.'

'You can really feel it, can't you? And this mightn't be the worst of it at all yet.'

'Or it might blow itself out in an hour or two. We're neither of us experts on storms, are we? For all we know, by mid-morning we could be sunbathing again.'

'Christ,' he said, trying to sound at ease, 'I love your optimism, sweetheart.'

'It's cold, isn't it?' She slipped back into the sleeping bag and curled herself just a moment against him then rolled onto her back and lay with her right arm raised and crooked above her head. 'Any idea what we can do to keep ourselves occupied?'

When he turned his face to her he saw that her eyes were a wide wet shine even in the tent's gloom and her mouth had thickened to the pout she always wore when trying to tease him into some game.

After some time had passed, Thomas was overcome by restlessness and got up and began to dress. When he sat to pull on his shorts, Isabelle reached out from the sleeping bag and caressed his back. His skin still held on to its wintry pallor, and nubs of bone marked the line and contours of his frame.

'You're not going out in that? Even if you don't get blown across onto the next island, you'll be a week trying to dry off.'

'I just want to take a look.'

'Are you mad? You can see well enough from the flap of the tent.'

'Also, I think I'd better check on the boat.'

She tried to remain calm. She could hear herself breathing.

'Well, if you're going then so am I.'

'There's no need, Izzy. I'll be ten minutes. You can stay here where it's nice and cosy. And when I get back it'll be your turn to find some way of heating me up.'

He turned, brought his mouth to hers and let the kiss linger. The quick dab of his tongue tipping against her own caused her to smile and then laugh. 'Go, if you're going,' she said, 'before I start ripping the clothes off you again.'

She watched him then, crouching to unfasten the tent flap, hesitating in the face of the outer storm and finally pushing himself forward, out into the morning's grey wash. Uncertainty stirred in her, and to counteract it she lay back once more on her pillow, closed her eyes and thought in a happy way about the hour they'd just passed.

When she opened her eyes again, nothing seemed to have changed. Rain still lashed against the tent, the light still bore the same leaden grey. But she was cold again, the parts of her that had remained exposed, her shoulders and her outstretched arm, almost numb. With difficulty, she sat up. In those few minutes, or however long it had been, there'd somehow been time for a nightmare. Snatches of it remained, filling her mind with wrong images, which made it a challenge to decipher reality; something about a small white dog, a Scotch terrier or some such similar breed, that arrived at the door of a house she'd never seen before but which, in her sleep-state, she apparently owned and called home. In his mouth, the dog carried, as a gift for her, the body of a pied wagtail. Blood reddened the dog's lips and teeth, so she assumed that the bird had been mauled and was dead, but once he'd dropped the little creature at her feet it began to stir, barely at first but then with increasing violence, trying in panic to flap its smashed wings. Through all of this, she did nothing but watch, and sometimes she watched the dog watching too. And then, suddenly, before she could even think of moving and just as the bird seemed set to recover and somehow fly away, the terrier leaned in, nudged the bird with his muzzle over onto its back and bit off its legs.

The whole thing had the quality of a nightmare, and yet she'd felt neither fear nor revulsion. In life she'd have wept for days after witnessing such horror, but in the dream she was quite untouched by the bird's suffering. After losing its legs it let out a terrible high-pitched noise, a single wavering note, and that, she thought, had probably just been the wind outside, its singing through the ruins of the shepherd's walls somehow penetrating the plot that her mind was unfurling. The bird lay there again, freshly destroyed, not moving but screaming, and then, pathetically, attempted once more and without the least success, to fly. She looked on, and so did the dog, and at last the dog got bored and turned and walked off, and then she too began to find the wagtail's efforts tiresome, and she lifted her foot and brought it down hard, twisting her heel against the threshold until nothing remained of the little life but a pulp of feathers and gore. Then she went back inside, wiped her feet on the mat, and closed the door.

Now she lay awake, still naked in the sleeping bag, helpless against a flood of dread. Thomas had said he'd be ten minutes, but surely it took longer than that to dream. She reached for her shorts and a T-shirt and, still huddled shivering beneath the covers, began to dress.

The rain came in sheets, and within seconds she was wet through. Away from the walls of the ruined cottage, the wind took full hold, a sweeping westerly that put everything at a hard slant. Isabelle braced herself and pushed headlong into the storm, blind to direction except in an instinctive way and perhaps guided too by a certain familiar footing within the ground's vague contours. Fighting into the wind, she called out repeatedly for Thomas, and even though it became quickly obvious that no words could penetrate this onslaught, she persisted in shouting, as if just feeling his name in her head and mouth could be enough to connect them. But nothing was moving behind the rain. And then, almost too soon, she found herself on the verge above their pocket of beach. Out ahead of her, somewhere, was the ocean, but sky and sea were one wetness this morning and only the faint white flashes of rupturing waves gave any semblance of balance to the morning.

From the little she could see, the beach below was empty. The rock wall and its side banks made a kind of cauldron of the land and the mesh of rain and tumbling waves smothered the little cove, so that details were hard to determine. At first she was sure that she could identify the shape of the boat close in near the foot of the cliff face, but the longer she looked the more her certainty weakened, and finally, just because she could think of nothing else to do or nowhere else to go, she decided to work her way down the path.

She hadn't time to realise her mistake. Over the past several days, the briar and fern had been trampled so repeatedly that it had flattened to a kind of carpet, but the night's deluge had turned everything slick. After a couple of steps she lost her footing, and slid and clattered on her back down the steep incline to within ten feet of the beach. A wedge of rock checked her forward momentum at some midway point, catching her a hard blow to the shoulder, and a glancing second shot to the head just above her left ear, and she came to a halt, finally, when she wrapped herself chest and midriff around a second, larger stump. There was no air to breathe then, and she shuddered and tried to cry out, but either the noise of the morning or the fire that had started inside her head, obliterating everything, crushed any sound she could make. And though she never quite lost consciousness, she did, for a time, lose the awareness of consciousness. Her mind just seemed to stop, and when it tuned itself in again, reluctantly, through a haze of static, the light had brightened a little and the rain had softened to a dense but more gentle mist. The least movement brought searing pain but she braced herself, spilt away from the rock and slid the last few yards down onto the sand. Slumped on one side, facing the water, she saw the ocean stacking waves away into the distance. In close to the shore they stood up to something approaching the height of a man, and broke, brushed for seconds at a time with foaming yellow-white crowns just before shredding themselves apart and rolling high up onto the beach. Further along, out where they hit the rocks, the crash was like trains colliding, and the spew climbed high up against the sheer cliff-sides, over and over, all with the relentless rhythm of a heartbeat, until the idea passed through her head that, if this should keep up, the island would surely find itself washed or worn away.

The sound of the sea filled her and made her feel small, but it was minutes before she realised that some of the whispering was internal and that she could hear nothing from her left ear. That side of her head felt split open, and when she reached to examine the wound felt a long flap of scalp and hair hanging down all the way to the corner of her jaw, and her fingers came away from their explorations drenched in blood that, as she watched and because of the mist, brightened and diluted itself down over her palm and wrist to almost nothing.

The head injury was deep and bad, she'd likely broken or at least badly bruised some ribs, and all down her back side, from her neck to her heels, the skin had been flayed and split to gaping by talons of briar. But the urge to just curl up and sleep was, she knew, a dangerous one. She had to move. The waves were huge and the tide was coming in, and if the storm hadn't yet blown itself out there could still be more and worse to come. The beach was not a place to be stranded. The effort of sitting up made her cry, and the tears that filled her eyes and spilt down her cheeks and into the corners of her mouth were the first hint of heat she'd known since leaving the tent. Pain rolled like gunshots through her head, and even the smallest stirring brought on a dizziness that threatened to put her out. But she wiped her eyes with a sandy wrist and looked around.

The beach was empty, the boat gone.

'Thomas,' she called again, in pure helplessness, lifting her voice as much as she could above the wind and holding her scratched and bleeding arms tightly across her middle, just beneath her breasts, in a largely futile bracing action. But there was no reply.

When she felt able, she walked the beach, taking each step carefully, testing her limits. The rock wall, which had hung forever above these and other ancient waves and which she had already seen lit up, screened in salt, under the hottest sun, now shone from the rain and the polish of the gales, hulking greyish sheets that looked to have been laid down by giant hands with some clear design in mind, the surface patched in white and yellow continents of lichen. At the wall's base, no hint of the boat remained, the sand long since washed and blown flat. Her initial assumption was that it must have slipped its mooring and been sucked down into the water, but then her mind threw up the possibility that Thomas might have come down here and taken it out in search of a better sheltering point. An experienced seaman would never have chanced the swell in such a flimsy vessel, but it was an explanation that made sense because, from what she'd seen, he was nowhere on the island.

Pressure had been building in her head, and now her vision began to blur. All noise faded into the distant background, and it was like being submerged in water and held under. A fresh wave of dizziness washed over her and set her trembling, and then the joints of her legs came loose and she dropped onto the sand and lay there, slumped over on herself, face down, one knee drawn up against her chest.

An hour later, Thomas found her.

After leaving the tent, and while she'd been asleep, he'd come to the beach to secure the boat. But the waves then were running huge and swamping the strand in great heaves, and leaving it simply tethered to a rock was surely all kinds of dangerous, especially with the tide coming in. Taking it out onto the water, though, seemed tantamount to suicide; and even if he could manage to avoid a capsize, finding a safer mooring place on the other side of the island was far from guaranteed. The only logical option was to haul it up the path and stow it safely inland. This idea at least was a sound one, but the effort it demanded was immense, taking nearly two hours, moving the vessel barely inches at a time and at alternating angles in an effort to keep it from sliding back to the bottom of the slope, and if the briar had helped supply a degree of traction then the hull's flat underbelly had so flattened the path as to make it, at least for the next few days, unusable. In the midst of his struggle, though, that seemed a trifling inconvenience. What mattered most was the safety of the boat, their lifeline.

The task was a relentless one, and had to be. Every step of taken hillside was hard earned, and he couldn't risk even a few seconds' rest, fearing a backslide. So once he and the boat made it to the relative safety of the top of the path, he collapsed down onto the soft wet grass. The rain then was still driving, but he was wet and dirty and no longer cared. He lay that way for a long time, with steam rising from his body, feeling the ache in his limbs and stretching occasionally in order to deepen the sense of it. Then, because drifting off into sleep became a real possibility, he roused himself and set off again, dragging the boat towards the nearest low point. And once he found what he adjudged to be a suitable dip in the ground, he capsized the vessel and made sure it was set fast and that the wind could in no way roll it.

He returned to the tent beaten and weary, ready to strip down, dry off with a towel and crawl back into bed, to sleep and wake and chat and laugh with Isabelle, leaving the storm around them to do its worst. But the tent was empty.

Panic flashed through him, but quickly passed. He knew what she was like, how she struggled to stand idle for long when left alone, and could never let such weather pass without getting outside to pleasure in its drama. With a deep sigh, he crawled back out, fastened the tent's flap again, and began to call her name.

At first he just walked, now and then calling out even though the wind collapsed his sound, making for the east end of the island, and for a while stood trying to glimpse some suggestion of the land across the reach. By now the rain had begun to ease, but aside from the wash of shadow in the distance that might have been Dunmore Head, there was nothing much at all to see, and Isabelle was nowhere around. He continued along in an aimless fashion, heedless by now of the rain but not yet really concerned either, not until he thought of something she'd said on one of the nights about the beach being Beginish's greatest surprise, that little perfect strand, the detail which had given her the most joy since they'd been here. The one part of the island that seemed to have been waiting for them to come along and discover.

Tired as he was, and barking out her name now, he broke into a run.

Within a minute he'd reached the rock ledge and because the wind had lessened was able to get right to the brink. Below on the sand, in near the sheer wall of stone and made ghostly by the mist, he could make out what looked to be Isabelle's shape. He called out to her repeatedly, and after a long, dead pause something down there stirred and he heard his own name spoken back small and frail.

'I'm coming down,' he shouted, and ran to the pathway with no thought now for his own safety. The speed of his descent helped, but only initially, and he managed to keep his footing until halfway down. Then he landed hard on his back, spun, and smashed head first into the large outcropping some fifteen feet from the bottom. Above him, the sky was falling gentle now as feathers into his face, and though he felt no pain and although the morning seemed to have turned suddenly quiet, a terrible coldness overcame his mind and he knew his neck was broken.

Isabelle had seen his fall and had even registered the sickening crunch of the collision. Her own pain instantly forgotten, she lifted herself up first onto her hands and knees and then, unsteadily, stood and staggered across to where he lay. Struggling up the path at a crawl and calling out for help that couldn't possibly come, she knelt beside him and stretched herself across his chest. Because she was crying, and perhaps also due to the effects of a concussion, her words were slurred and, apart from the pleading repetition of his name, largely unrecognisable. He stared past her, unable yet to speak, and wept too, warm tears that built and in their bursting dissolved all focus. She'd never known him not to be strong, and now her own fear deepened, but she used a thumb to wipe the tears away then leaned in and kissed his eyes, whispering and whimpering all the time that the situation probably wasn't as bad as it seemed and that, if they only rested here for a while, an hour or two, maybe, they'd be all right.

The wind had dropped but the waves continued to build, and they lashed the beach with an appetite for ground, huge breakers that thickened and burst in sheets up along the strand. Though the high-tide line stopped roughly at the bottom of the path, the storm's surge seemed likely to set a new mark, one that could even potentially engulf them where they perched, and Thomas strained to work out how high the water would come and how long they'd have but with his mind shutting down his focus refused to hold on anything for more than a few seconds before been overtaken by a sweep of other thoughts and memories. Older doors, especially, were swinging open, and he kept returning to how it had been as a child, after he'd tumbled from a tree or off a wall or after he'd been badly on the losing side of some fight, and the terror of knowing that damage was done, a creeping numbness that made other details drop away. Broken fingers, a broken nose, teeth knocked loose, tetanus shots from stepping on the rusty nails that littered building sites, wounds that needed stitching, knee or head gashes usually, but once his chin and, another time, most painfully, his tongue, after he'd bitten it nearly in two while jumping from a shed roof. The biggest thing then, just as much as the actual injury, was having to tell his mother, because of how she'd weep at seeing him hurt, and the scene she'd make, even in the hospital, shouting and threatening him with what his father would do when he got home, and at the same time smothering him with a hurricane of kisses and hugs that would have the young nurses bowing their heads or turning away in order to hide their smirks. And there'd been the time when, at twelve years old, he'd gone skinny-dipping with some of the other kids from school and broken his ankle jumping off a low bridge into the river, because somebody had dumped a shopping trolley in the murky water. That one had required surgery, the insertion of two pins and a steel plate to reconstruct the bone, and everyone, even the doctors, had said how lucky he was to have gone in that way, because if it had been a head-first dive then he'd likely not have survived. For years after, he'd suffered nightmares about what happened, about hitting the water and not immediately going under, and then keeling sideways in a stupor of pain and nearly drowning because his lungs had filled so quickly. When he regained consciousness in the ambulance, they had him muzzled with oxygen, and they were almost at the hospital before he realised that his clothes had been left back on the bridge, his T-shirt, jeans and boxer shorts neatly folded on top of his running shoes. Until this new fall, the broken ankle had been his most serious injury, and his mind now held on to the absurd thought that at least this time he was clad.

'You're hurt,' he whispered to Isabelle, when he could form words again, and she stared at him, seemingly lost, then reached to delicately fingertip her head wound. Even with the mist, blood had matted the hair and stained nearly to blackness the entire left side of her face. 'What happened to you?'

'I fell. I was looking for you and I fell.' She sounded drunk, that same stunned blur of a voice, and the effect intensified when an unaccountable bleat of laughter bubbled up through her tears. 'The boat's gone. I thought you'd left me.'

'The boat.' He inhaled with effort. 'I moved it.' Whispering, then: 'Up the path. It's safe.'

'I was afraid you'd rowed away in the storm.'

'Never,' he said, trying hard to smile. The light now was growing dim and he tried to think about how much time had passed, how many hours, and whether it was possible that evening could have already settled. But the logic eluded him and, above and all around, the day continued to fade. 'I'll never leave you, Izzy. You have me for good.'

She wept harder then, kissed his mouth and face, and telling him in sobs how much she loved him and how she'd been born for him, how they'd been born for one another, she lay her head down on his chest and shoulder in an awkward half-embrace. Unable to move or respond, his stare contemplated how the little remaining wind, thick with mist, made shapes in the air. And after some time, when it just seemed easier to do so, and against the constant, soothing backdrop of his wife's sad words, he gave in and let his eyes slip shut.

'Tom?' she whispered, once she realised that he was no longer awake. Then, louder: 'Tommy, everything will be fine. I promise it will. It has to be. Can you hear me, Tommy?'

He moaned, and it was a sign of life but nothing more, and she sat up and considered him and the way that he was lying and then the waves spilling in barely ten feet below now, coming up to the bottom of the track in soapy rushes and trailing back again, but trailing back a little less with each new flourishing spill. And yards out, the big waves continued to build and roll, and the sea, having turned glassy over a deeper grey and lit up with a kind of cruel hardness away in the distance, was a war that she understood would just keep on coming.

Her own head pounded, not just from the burn of the wound but with some deeper and more considered hurt, and the pain was still fresh in her chest and ribs when she made the least movement. Yet as significant as these injuries were, and as hard as it was to make any sense at all of what had happened, her agonies needed to be put aside. Survival was all that mattered now.

Kissing him a final time, shuddering at the coldness of his mouth and the earthy taste that had turned his breath so sour, she turned away, set herself and began to clamber up the path, oblivious now to the claws of briar that punctured and ripped open the skin of her palms, knees and shins, moving with care, dreading a misstep that would spill her again, watching only the hacked and battered ground beneath her hands. When she finally reached the top the urge to stretch out and rest was immense, but she forced herself on and broke into a staggering, lopsided run, and within a couple of minutes was back in the tent, rummaging through their rucksacks for the rain capes, a dry wool blanket and the plastic covering sheets that would at least shield him, if he absolutely had to spend the night where he lay, from the worst of what the storm might bring. Thoughts as to the magnitude of his injury pressed at her mind but she pushed them away, not yet ready to face them or to admit to herself how serious the situation had become. As soon as the rain stopped, she'd attempt a fire, and if necessary she'd burn everything they possessed in the hopes of attracting the attention of someone on the mainland. Even the boat, if it came to that. For now, though, given that Thomas was in no fit condition to be moved, she resolved to stay on the path with him. Whatever was to come, whether freak waves or lightning strikes, they'd deal with it together.

*

After the rain, which had finally given way at some point in the night, dawn broke cold and clear. Isabelle woke reluctantly, her head slamming, her whole body full of chill beneath her plastic blanket. Thomas hadn't stirred since his eyes slipped shut those few minutes after his fall and, even with the wool blanket pressed tightly to his body beneath his own waterproof covering, his skin felt perished to the touch. Stars were bright in those patches where the cloud had split apart, and even with the sun on the first of its rise away in the east, darkness continued to cloak the sheltered beach. Down below, it was just possible to make out the phosphorescent breaking of waves that, having spent their ire, had already begun to settle.

Stretching away the night's stiffness caused such a stabbing sensation in her chest that a surge of tears welled suddenly, but she understood that her pain meant little, even the head wound that was probably by now past stitching and would likely leave her marked for life. All she could do, at this point, was start a fire and pray that somebody across on the mainland would notice her signalling for help.

Deciding on a plan brought a modicum of peace. She clambered back up the slope, and at the tent began to gather anything that could be set to burn. They had some driftwood put by, and remembering how Thomas had used seaweed to get their evening fires lit, she emptied her rucksack and over the next few hours returned again and again to the beach, where she collected all the old dead ropes of it she could find. Everything was sodden from the storm, but her intention was to get a small fire going first, and to lay out the kelp close to the flames in order to bake it dry.

After a quick consideration, she settled on a small dip in the ground about twenty paces from the island's easternmost side, facing Dunmore Head and the beach from which they'd set out, and began to stack her wood. The fire needed to blaze for as long as possible. Their only hope now – certainly the only hope that Thomas had – lay with rescue.

But even the small fire she set in order to dry out the kelp refused to take the flame. She persisted, trying for more than an hour to coax it awake, and by then the sun was already well into its climb and the morning had once more begun to swelter.

Not knowing what else to do, and telling herself that the seaweed would dry out naturally now and of its own accord, she hurried back to the path. She could see from the ridge that Thomas was as she'd left him, still upside down among the briar and cocooned in his wool and plastic wrappings. And smiling instead of giving in again to tears, she inched her way down the slope and crouched at his side. He looked the way he so often did when, on summer mornings, she'd woken early and just lay there in their small rented bed, watching him sleep. Breath sifted in and out of his body in such shallowness as to be imperceptible, and his face, relaxed, seemed just a layer of skin removed from the boy he'd so recently been. Though she rarely gave credence to the existence of a God any more, she'd often spent minutes of those bright, twilit dawns considering the convoluted hindsight destinies which had somehow steered them each across the other's path, and in that found herself allowing again for the possible existence of an Almighty. Even if her belief only ever held for those early minutes and was always quickly lost to the attrition of the rising day, the idea that life, in all its seeming confusion and turmoil, had already been mapped out ahead of them proved strangely comforting then, the assurance that nothing was quite as random as it seemed and that there really was some greater purpose to it all. Now, again, she clung to such a notion, and insisted to herself that if fate truly was for anything more than fairy tales then there was no way that this could be the end, because what God would take the trouble to design something as complex as a life, with all its forked paths and unpredictable intersections, simply for it to run such a futile course? No, this wouldn't be the finish; there'd be more to come, and in time they'd look back and laugh about or at least roll their eyes over such folly. Sitting here now and studying Thomas, she considered what stories his mind in sleep might be unfurling, and rubbing his cheek gently with her dirty fingertips, feeling the scrub of beard that had in recent days taken proper hold, wished only happiness for his dreams. Then, overcome again with love, she stooped to kiss his lips. The sourness that had filled his mouth last night seemed to have deepened and turned rotten, and his lips were cold as raw meat, but she held herself to him and uttered reassurance and oaths of devotion against his teeth and frozen tongue.

Too often, she knew, her tendency was to live either among memories of days that had passed or in fantasies about what might lie ahead, and always at a cost of the true moment. Breathing was the trick that Thomas had taught her, though actually he was just as guilty of such wishful indulgence. But she practised now what she'd learned, working against her pain with long, unsteady breaths, in through the nose, out through the mouth, repeating the process until the present once again began to shine, heightening reality to its rightful level. The waves had dropped, and within a minute she'd eased herself down the last few feet of slope and was naked, taken by this sudden, irresistible urge to strip away her dirty clothes, and stretched out on the soft sand just where the water lapped at the shoreline in nothing more than foamy whispers. Once she'd settled, the low waves came barely against her, cool fingers and tongues that numbed and thrilled with each caress, but now and then a slightly greater surge spilt the tide up over her entirely, submerging her for the one-two punch of a heart's slamming before drawing back again. Her wounded skin burned with the bite of the salt, and though the stinging at first made her gasp and clench her teeth, gradually it became almost pleasurable, and her mind filled up with a sense of healing. The water swept in and over her, the rushing coldness causing her flesh to prickle, her nipples to tighten into small knots, and everything stopped and her head filled with noise, a single booming hush, and for that instant she felt herself on the fringe of a second state of being, a dense, murky, slow-motion existence as true as the one which lay above the waves. Then, once again, she was in the open, squeezing her eyes nearly completely shut against the glare and gasping at the day that closed down on her like a hot blanket.

After a while, she got up, washed her shorts and T-shirt in the surf and lay them out on the rocks to dry. Always, Thomas was in sight, never more than twenty or thirty paces away, and apart from the strangeness of his pose, inverted as he was on the incline and pillowed against the stub of rock, it was easy to imagine him as simply asleep. At home, she'd often chat to him while he slept, especially of a Sunday morning when he'd drifted back into a lazy doze in the aftermath of love, and on those occasions she'd talk just to put a sound in the room, keeping to nothing subjects, the conversation suited to a one-sided shape since the questions she asked were little more than air and echoes anyway. Seeing him now, it seemed easy enough to keep that same game going.

'You know what we should get, Tommy? A dog. I'd like a dog, I think. But not something small, not one of those poor things that have to live in a purse. Something normal-looking. A Border collie, maybe. They're a loyal breed, and intelligent, not to mention beautiful. They have such handsome faces, don't you think? Kind of old, as if they already know you and all about you. Even as pups, they're like that. We'd have to get a bigger place of course, and we'd need a garden, or at least a yard, because it'd be cruel to keep a dog like that boxed in, but we'll have to find somewhere new to live anyway when we get back, so these are things we should probably be thinking about.'

As she talked, she leaned against the rock wall and felt with the fingers of both hands the cuts and slashes striping and criss-crossing her entire back side. Some were particularly deep, and sore: one high up on her right leg, another at an angle across both cheeks of her bottom, and a third just beneath her right shoulder blade; but these were merely the most significant of the superficial wounds, and there was hardly an inch of her body from neck to ankles that stretched unmarked. These cuts and scratches, though, would at least heal, given time. More serious was the pain that continued to dig into her right side, and the skin from her breast down to the jut of her pelvis was clouded a deep, angry red that looked as if blood had seeped from something precious within and corroded the flesh without penetrating the skin. It ached still to stretch, or even to walk, and she was so tender to the touch that even an accidental rubbing reduced her to tears. The ribs were almost certainly broken, but from the little she knew of such injuries she understood that the only treatment was rest.

'Give it a chance. That's what my mother used to say. The body knows itself. That's probably why yours has you sleeping so much. You'll probably wake up ready to run races. Maybe you'll need a few more hours, or even a day or two, but there's no hurry on us, is there? And as soon as the seaweed dries out, I'll get the fire lit. It shouldn't be long now. The sun is already strong. And somebody will come. That was a bitch of a storm, though, wasn't it? At one point, I thought we'd wake up in Oz. But we're still here. It's a good little island, all things considered. Beginish. Even the name is nice to say. Sad, that all of these places stand deserted, don't you think? But if there were still people here then I suppose that would have been reason enough for us not to come.'

Her clothes, even after a couple of hours on the rocks, were still damp to the touch. The ocean lay spread out before her, beautiful now in its colouring, cracklings of light sun-dropping the blueness. Off to her left, but hidden by the jut of the beachhead, lay the Great Blasket, and she wondered whether the morning's tourists had yet arrived there, and whether or not the ferry, in returning, would come close enough for her to possibly catch their attention. But instead of rushing off to survey the situation, she went again to sit a while beside Thomas, and settling herself cross-legged on the sheet that had served as her protection through the night, she loosened his bindings but left in place the woollen blanket. Again, she kissed him and found his mouth and the flesh of his cheek cold as lead to her lips.

'I'm going to have another try at getting the fire lit,' she said finally. 'And I suppose I'd better put some clothes on, just in case someone does come. A glimpse of me dancing around in the skinny might lure them onto the rocks. Or scare them away.' She smiled at him as if he could see and was watching her, then returned to the tent and dressed in her spare shorts, pink denims that came in shreds nearly to her knees, and an old sleeveless blue linen blouse. With the sun shining, the morning seemed to have stagnated. Nothing moved anywhere, apart from a couple of huge Atlantic gulls circling like kites high above the water away to the north. The belts of seaweed strung out on the grass had at last begun to dry, though the heavier ones were still clammy, and she used what she could, bedding the most brittle pieces in beneath the chunks of driftwood, adding a few twisted pages from the end of *A Political History of the Middle East*, one of three or four books they'd squeezed into their rucksacks in case they ever found themselves overcome by boredom. The paper caught fire quickly, lapping up the match's small orange flame, and some of the more thinly cut slices of wood also began to burn. The kelp only smoked, bluish-grey ribbons initially, which soon thickened into a defined charcoal column, and although she'd hoped for a hard blaze, even an inferno, she decided that this was fine, too, because smoke could usually be seen from quite a distance and was at least as likely as the sight of flames to get them noticed. Yet within minutes the smaller pieces of wood burned themselves out without having more than singed the larger chunks, and soon after that the smoke from the kelp thinned out to nothing. She'd been stooped in a crouch to one side of the bonfire, and as it died she felt such a surge of despair that she cried out. In panic, she tried feeding more kelp in among the smouldering wood, but far from reinvigorating the blaze her efforts only served to quicken the extinguishing.

Tears once again squeezed up into her eyes, and she angrily wiped them away with the heels of her scratched palms, then sat back on the grass, felt it pressing damp into the seat of her shorts, and stared across at the mainland, at the thin strip of beach and the grey knuckle of Dunmore Head. But the whole scene was a picture. Nothing moved anywhere.

Giving in, of course, was not an option, and she understood that her only chance was to try again, and to keep trying until the last shred of combustible material had been spent. But instead of immediately doing so, she got up and walked a slow lap of the island, surveying the water on every side, not with expectation but perhaps in the hope, however forlorn, of finding inspiration. The day continued to sweat, and off to the east harmless scratches of cloud laid shadowy hints across the hard-lit water, creating the illusion of large, barely submerged shoals or some behemoth set to break the surface.

She'd just settled to the fire again and was tearing more pages from the back of the history book, still with her eyes cast casually back towards Dunmore Head, when a rowboat appeared from one such stripe of greyness. Her mind tried to make sense of what she was seeing without quite believing a line of it, but the second split and her pulse began to race hard and then to pound until she felt fit to burst, and though the boat was surely still too far out, half a mile or more yet, she got to her feet and ran right to the grassy cusp and began to shout and wave her arms above her head.

*

Ten or fifteen minutes later, she was waist-deep in the sea, helping to drag the boat in onto the strand.

The wait, now that help was so near, had been interminable, and she'd suffered one mad, frightening moment when she felt certain the boatman was just going to pass by, and she hurt herself badly in the nearly berserk effort of shouting and waving, trying to make herself obvious, until her right side burned and turned her faint, but even as she'd begun to wilt the rower raised a hand in greeting, and with several hard pulls on the oars brought himself in close to the rocks.

'Did you see my fire?' she asked, her voice flapping with shock. 'Was that it? Was that why you came?'

Across the span of the boat, Paudie Joe watched her, trying to understand. She looked as if she'd taken a few hours of the worst kind of beating, the flesh around her eyes hanging in blue hammocks, her head split open, crusts of blood dreadlocking her hair down her right side. He could hear pain in the higher notes of her struggling words.

'Fire? No, girl. I didn't see a fire. But if you managed to get one lit after all that rain then you're a better hand with a few sticks than I am. No, it's the storm that has me out here. To tell you the truth, I was a bit worried. We got a fair battering even over on the mainland, and I just wanted to check that you hadn't been washed away.'

They got the boat onto the sand and let it rock over into a starboard lean.

And then he saw Thomas.

'He fell,' Isabelle said, in explanation. Her bones felt suddenly soft, and fatigue pulled her into the beginnings of a stoop. 'He'd come out to check on the boat. When he was gone a while, I went looking for him, but the rain and wind made it so hard to see. I fell trying to come down the slope there, and hurt myself on a couple of rocks. I hit my head and I think I've probably broken a few ribs. All I could do for a long while was curl up on the sand. Some time after, I don't know how long, he came and found me. But Christ, that path.'

'When did this happen?'

'I don't know. Yesterday at some stage. In the morning, I think.'

'And has he been out the whole time?'

She looked at where Thomas lay. Now that they were safe, terror stirred in the deepest part of her stomach. 'No,' she said. 'No, he was awake at first. And he had no pain. Then he slept, and I thought that was probably best, that it'd give his body a chance to heal, you know. I got us blankets and plastic sheets, and we spent the night on the path there. There was nothing else I could have done. Maybe I could have dragged him down onto the beach, but the tide was coming in and the waves were huge. And then, this morning, I thought about moving him again, but I was afraid of doing even more damage.' She let out a long sigh, and when she could speak again sounded very young, and in need. 'Do you think he'll be all right?'

Paudie Joe let the question hang. After a hesitation, he fumbled among the contents that littered the bottom of the boat, found a bottle of water and a sandwich wrapped in brown paper. He held them out for her and she took them and let her stare follow as he started away for the path. From where she stood, she saw him clamber up the slope, stoop beside Thomas and, after a moment, bless

89

himself. He hung there, unmoving, his face close to the rock, before eventually lifting his head again and considering her, the boat and the beach.

'So, what do we do?' she asked, when he came back down onto the sand. 'Do we move him?'

His eyes, nested in flesh, were slits and couldn't seem to focus. Every few seconds he lifted his cap and ran a flat hand across his greased hair. His mouth twitched.

'We don't,' he said, his voice rattling. He cleared his throat and began to dig in his pockets for a cellphone. 'I'd say we need to leave him be.'

*

The inquest was, at least with regard to the law, a formality. Death by misadventure. Five weeks after she'd escaped Beginish, Isabelle had to sit on a raised chair in a room more like a school classroom than a court, and answer a litany of questions, but by then she'd already been a dozen times through everything that could possibly be asked, and nobody pushed her too hard.

But months on, and even now, some four years later, there were mornings still – more often than not, actually – when she woke with the dawn to the certain feel of Thomas beside her. When that happened, she'd lie there listening and recollecting, straining for the sense of him unsettling the dark, and in those moments she'd either keep her eyes shut or fix her stare tightly on the ceiling and indulge in the memory of stretching out for his hand, or rolling against him and reaching across his chest for the faraway flap of his heartbeat. As everything turned real, she wept, on and on until dawn whitened the walls around her, minutes that passed soundless except for the inner sobbing of a tide and the remembered promises of his hushed voice breezing against her skin when he brought himself to her with all his uttered talk of love and beauty, all the gasping assurances of forever, and all words that left her carved open and hollowed with despair.

And when, on towards seven, the alarm began to ring, she'd knock it silent and remain a moment longer, wide awake in a bed and an apartment that he had never occupied, before getting up, the loneliness alive and strong within her, to dress ahead of yet another day.

# Love is Strange

Miss Reilly, who was probably in her seventies when I knew her, had never married. I remember asking my sister, Bríd, about that, and she said that Lizzie Reilly wasn't the kind of woman men wanted as a wife. Bríd was a year and a half older than me and, at fifteen, had taken to sneering at everything. 'The wrong kind of ways, you might say,' she explained, and did something knowing with her mouth. In those days, all her stories dropped away only half told. In silence, I watched her small fingers, with the nails bitten deep into the flesh and painted an ugly, flaking scarlet, pick a needle and thread through the high-risen hem of her best skirt, and tried hard not to stare at the bare flesh of her exposed thighs. 'You'll understand eventually,' she added, with one of those put-upon sighs that she believed to be womanly as opposed to girlish.

Whenever I passed Miss Reilly on the road, I tried to see her as the woman she must once have been. The fact that she had nothing in old age to mark her out as particularly ugly, no disfigurements or skewed features, meant surely that neither could they have existed during her youth and prime. Coppery tufts of hair bracketed her slatted mouth, but a little grooming would have cleared that deck in a hurry, and far uglier women than her had found men to share their burdens.

By that time, '61 and into '62, the rust having long since set in, the Miss Reilly I saw most days shuffling through Douglas village was already stooped and halfway broken. Generally reeking with alchemical infusions of pipe tobacco and liniment, and with mauve or pinkish curls spooling out from beneath the lifted peak of a paisley-patterned headscarf, her shape was usually set lopsided by a string-woven carrier bag laden with pint bottles of Beamish stout, a loaf of batch bread, and tins of meat or sardines that would go mostly to her cats.

If I happened to be out on the street I'd abandon what-ever game I had going and run to her with an offer of assistance. If she was tired, as she usually was, if the heat and pollen were getting to her or if the winter's damp had put an ache deep into her hips and knees, she'd wordlessly accept, and I'd take the bag and we'd walk together, I having to check my step to keep pace with her, up through the village and halfway up Donnybrook Hill to the little range of terraced hovels where she'd been born. Until the previous summer she had shared the house with her brother, Séamus, who'd also never married and who'd years earlier lost an arm in a mill accident. I remember him as a quiet sort, usually three-quarters of the way drunk, no matter what the time of day, but muted from it rather than fired up, as some tended to get, dragging himself back from the post office or the pub in the direction of home, with his right shirtsleeve knotted at its elbow and his mouth always chewing on the silent words of some half-remembered song or prayer. One morning in late July, Miss Reilly found him cold in his bed, and some of the kids who lived along the row from her said that the doctor, when he came, was forced to dig nearly elbow-deep down the corpse's throat for the palate of false teeth that had been swallowed in the struggle for those final few breaths. Now the old woman was on her own, but her life went on as it always had.

None of the other kids ever offered to help carry her things, at least not that I can remember. I don't know why I did, or why I liked her. At that age, I'm not sure what I knew. But she was old and looked so much in the want of help, and even if there'd been nothing else then that would have been enough.

'Hurry, Sam,' one of the boys would say, if she happened along while we were kicking a ball around, or playing glassy alleys, or just sitting on the kerb, going on about school or dogs or whatever John Wayne film we'd seen at the Assembly Rooms the few weeks before. Kelleher, usually, or McNamara. They always had the biggest mouths for mockery, and the stupidity to either miss or else not care a damn about the line they were crossing. 'Your girlfriend is coming. Tell us, does the moustache tickle when she kisses you? Then again, maybe that's what you like about her. Don't you think she looks a bit like one of the Mexicans out of *The Magnificent Seven*?' At first, I let them tease, but that proved a mistake because eventually a few of the girls from our terrace overheard and started making me their entertainment, and to stop it I had to take on Kelleher in the yard one day after school, Kelleher because he had probably ten inches in height on McNamara and almost as much on me, and I split his lip and made his nose bleed but let him get in a couple of knocks too, so that it would look more evenly balanced than it actually was and so that we could again be friends later on. And after that, the teasing mostly ceased.

Miss Reilly never offered much in the way of gratitude, though sometimes she'd smile – a sad, distant kind of expression which would leave her so nearly overcome that she'd have to sit or else lean against some piece of furniture. 'You're a good boy,' she'd say, on those occasional days when her mind focused enough to let her remember my name, and I'd laugh and tell her that she was about the only one who thought so, because my teacher certainly didn't, and my mother often suggested, usually after I'd done something lousy, which was about forty times a week and double that during the summer, that I didn't belong to her at all, that I'd been switched at birth by the faeries.

'She doesn't mean it,' Miss Reilly would tell me. 'People say things like that all the time. What we say isn't always what we mean, especially to loved ones.'

I'd shrug, because I was actually fine with the idea that I might have magical blood, no matter how wicked, and when things began to turn awkward, when the silence of the house took us over, I'd clear my throat, say, 'Well, so long,' and take my leave before she'd start to think I was waiting for something more, that I was expecting a reward of some kind. I wasn't. It's difficult to explain. I could say that it was because my father had put manners into me, that he'd taught me to respect the elderly, even if he never taught me much else. And that was certainly part of it. But the truth was, I simply liked being around her. She interested me, and I enjoyed her company.

At thirteen I had started to feel a push to my horizons, and she represented one of the sides of the world as it existed beyond myself. If she was a parcel of blood and bones now then she still contained a wealth of thoughts, fears and memories, and maybe old laughter, too. I had a sense that time, even for the likes of her, was full in ways I couldn't yet begin to know. When I looked I saw the etchings of mistakes, and the creases and marbling of disappointment, but when I peered close I also saw past them to the crowding shadows of chances taken and missed. Though I had little understanding then of what it all meant, I nonetheless sensed its significance, and it matters even more so now as I slip into the tallow bloom of my own old age.

\*

'What are you playing at?' Bríd asked me, one evening, probably of an August or September, given the quality of the light that brightens my recollection: the faded gold of a summer nearing its end. I was in the copper tub, hunched up in front of the fireplace in maybe five inches of water, trying to hide my young nakedness. She'd come in and just stood there, hands on hips, staring down at me, that familiar little smirk squeezing her lips. My father was on a late shift at the Mill; my mother was in the backyard, hanging out clothes on the line after a day spent washing.

'What do you mean?'

'Don't come the innocent. You're up to something.'

'Would you mind turning around, please?'

'Why? It's not as if you have much worth seeing. And anyway, that water is filthy. I've eaten clearer soup. You'd be better off washing in the river.'

'What do you want, Bríd?'

She put one foot on the bathtub's rim and set both hands onto her raised knee. I tried not to look up, and instead stared at how the sandal's fraying leather thong separated her big toe from the rest. As usual, she'd painted her nails, a few crimson dabs that she'd coaxed from one of her friends, most likely Anna, who always had a ready supply because of a sister, the eldest of the Sweeney girls, living in Wolverhampton. I had a little bit of a thing for Anna, probably of all the girls in the village, because she was a couple of years older than me and because her straight waist-length hair made me think of the Apache women in the cowboy films I'd seen. And I loved that she called me Sam, the way my family did, and the closest of my friends, instead of Sammy, which was who I was to everyone else.

'I want to know,' Bríd said, lowering her voice a notch so that the sound would not carry out into the backyard, 'why you're hawking around Lizzie Reilly.'

'I'm not hawking.'

'Yes you are. Don't bother denying it. The whole place is talking. And I've seen you myself. Carrying her bag up the hill for her. Everyone who knows you knows you're rotten through, so you must be smearing it on like lard for her. What are you after? Sweets? Money?'

'She's an old woman. That bag is too much for her to be lifting. That's all. And I don't mind. I like coming back down the hill after. If you run fast enough you feel like you're losing all control. You feel like you're about to take off.' I glanced up at her, but with the hem of her skirt gaping I caught a pinkish hint of underwear, and I looked away quickly, crouched further forward and drew my knees up towards my chest so that nothing could happen. 'Not you, of course. People who are actually capable of running, I mean.'

'Is she paying you? Is that it?'

'No.'

'Because I need six shillings. We can call it a loan. Anna said her sister can get us Mystic Nylons and the six bob will even cover the cost of postage.'

'She isn't paying me.'

I could feel my sister watching me, but refused to look up. Finally, she removed her foot and squatted down so that she was on her haunches beside me. She held on to the rim of the bath for balance, and though she didn't have the strength to move it something about this disturbance caused a little water to slop out over the side. The flagstone floor around the bath darkened.

'If you're holding out,' she said, bringing her voice down to just above a whisper and filling it with menace, 'if you've got a stash, I'll find it. And then you'll have nothing. But if you gave me the six shillings I'd never bother you about the rest. And I'd make it up to you.'

Out through the open door onto the yard, our mother was almost to the end of the line. A breeze was causing our vests and my father's shirts to sway. I couldn't help myself. I turned and met Bríd's stare. She was serious, and trying to be sweet, but her eyes were wide and green without the sheen of direct light, and I could see the tension pulling at the muscles of her face.

'How?' I whispered, my mouth suddenly dry.

Her lips tightened at their corners. 'Don't ask stupid questions,' she said. 'Are you going to give me the money or not?'

'If I had money,' I said, 'I'd give it to you. But I don't. Swear and cross my heart. Not a ha'penny. Miss Reilly doesn't pay me. I don't look for anything from her.'

The clench of her teeth caused her jaw to twitch hard behind its flesh. I knew without having to turn my head that, out in the yard, our mother was nearly done with the clothes. Bríd knew, too, because she pulled on her meanest smile, her final jab before the surrender. 'Anna thinks you must have a thing for the old bitch. I told her that even if you had you'd be backing the wrong dog. Even the little you have going, the very little, would be too rich for dear Elizabeth.'

*

I finished with school that year. I made my Confirmation in March of '62, and in early June, the day after we broke up for the summer, I started work in the Mill. A boy's wages, but still, earning money. My father had already spoken with Tadhgie Burke, and even though you had to be fourteen in those days to get a start and I wouldn't have been of an age until that October, they'd arranged it so that I wasn't to be asked for papers and such until a week after the correct date. Our village had its own way of setting rules and settling accounts. Room was made for me within its walls, but it also locked me in.

For a while, Miss Reilly was there, the same as everyone else, as part of the casual background. And then, for me, she simply slipped out of the picture. I'm not sure why I can't recall the last time I was in her home or spoke a few words to her on the road, but I suppose endings only reveal themselves with the benefit of hindsight, and I'd have had no cause, in actually living those moments, to mark them out as in any way special.

In the Mill I spent my days shoulder-deep in grime, alongside grown men; I rolled cigarettes and smoked with them during lunch breaks and smiled and even laughed at the teasing things they talked about, their voices hushed and crackling like gravel under running feet, their eyes flashing for the room's corners and across the floor to make certain that there were no women or girls within earshot, and if I understood little apart from the lowness of their words I still felt my way along, the way all the lads of my age did, learning my lessons until the mysteries started to unravel. Work was everything then, swallowing days and leaving you so tired that, after the short walk home at the end of your shift, and slouched in a shallow stupor, you ate the bit of dinner that your mother put up for you, your mind having already dropped to a slower speed, and then sat for a couple of hours by the fire or, if the evening was a fine one, outside to stand a while with whoever was around, and you went to bed early so that you'd be up the following morning, bright and ready for more of the same.

Against all of that, the weekend was an interlude in reality, a day and a half's worth of time that afforded an extra hour's sleep and which got to be spent playing hurling or running drag hunts, with Kelleher, who'd also gone into the Mill, McNamara, who was serving a carpentry apprenticeship under his mother's brother, and some interchangeable handful of the dozen or so other lads that we'd known forever, that we'd climbed trees and fought and sang and laughed and come out of school with. And Saturday night, once we'd all found our appetites, was for dancing.

I recall the big night out as being part of an almost weekly routine in the same way I remember long hot summers and perfect snow-clad Christmas Eves, but that's just how my ageing mind works, living for diamond moments plucked from the otherwise incessant drabness. In fact, we probably only got to indulge our hormones once every couple of months, if even that often, travelling by bus the ten miles down to the Majorca in Crosshaven and usually walking the ten miles back, the late hour be damned, happy to be saving the shilling's fare and fuelled by passed-around bottles of stout, our heads swimming with rock 'n' roll beats and the thoughts of those girls who had let us take them out on the floor to swing beneath the over-amplified howling of Brendan Bowyer and the Royal Showband, or Butch Moore and the Capitol.

I couldn't help but change. Life demanded it. I grew up, set my sights in different directions and answered different needs. I made no conscious decision to step away from Miss Reilly, or from any of the details that had comprised my childhood; it was simply that my ear attuned itself to other callings. Bríd was still at home, and if anything changing only for the worse, her voice airy from having to so constantly speak down to lesser intellects, her eyes always a flicker away from a superior roll, and yet still existing to taunt, flirt and antagonise, but because of work, and my own occasional play, I saw less of her and her friends, and even when I stayed in of an evening she was usually off somewhere, leading some Blackrock or Passage boy astray with promises that she had no intention of fulfilling.

And then, somewhere around my sixteenth birthday, after months of watching from afar and a few awkward attempts at conversation, Sally Donovan agreed to come out for a walk with me. It's still like yesterday in my mind, the Carrigaline Road of a bright early evening, unexpectedly fine for so deep into autumn even with little more than the memory of a sun remaining in the sky, and she in a navy-blue skirt to her knees, tight-fitting yellow wool cardigan with the top button undone and the sleeves pushed up her forearms, and her wheaten hair in a swept-back shoulder-length wave that, to my eyes, made her look just like Grace Kelly.

I'd told nobody about the date, but at the last minute had confided in my father, and he laughed at first and started to tease me but then, understanding, I suppose, grew suddenly serious. He went to his pocket for the handkerchief in which he kept his few coins but, because it was still only Wednesday, all he could do was advise that I walk on the outside of the footpath, which was the gentlemanly thing to do where girls and women were concerned. 'Just make sure to behave yourself, boy,' he added, looking at me in an open way that was unusual for him, he being the shy sort even with us. 'I know you will anyway, but it wouldn't do to turn forgetful. Jack Donovan is a sound enough fella, but he'd feed you to the dogs over one of his daughters. And he'd be well within his rights.'

Sally and I had known one another our entire lives; I'd played with her brothers, and with her, too, out on the Pond Bank, damming the river of a summertime so that we could deepen it enough to swim. But because she was that year or so younger than me, and because a year at seven or eight or ten was a chasm, she hadn't stuck in my mind the way others did. And if anything, having shared a childhood only intensified our awkwardness.

Hardly a word passed between us until we reached Carr's Hill, though I was tuned tight to every step she took. Dead leaves from the sycamore and horse-chestnut trees that crowded the road on either side whispered and crunched beneath our feet; the stripped branches, tangled together above us, intensified the gold-white stabs of penetrating light; and occasional pecks of breeze, whenever we reached a clearing, put strands of hair across her face. For us, being so young, those were moments of deep romance, and for me, anyway, but I think for Sally, too, there'd never again be such a heightened sense of awareness, such a feeling of having stepped between life stages and tasting, even if only as a sip, the astonishment of immortality. All along the way, until the tree cover cleared and the great iron cross of the paupers' graveyard loomed into view, she kept stealing glances at me that I pretended not to notice, apart from once or twice when our eyes couldn't help but meet and which she answered with an embarrassed grin.

She'd already told me, just as we were setting out, that she had to be home before teatime, that her father would be at my door if she wasn't. For that reason, we decided that the top of Carr's Hill was far enough, and because we still had time and because it was so quiet and peaceful out here, we sat a while on a ditch, side by side and looking out across fields that I knew well, some from having hunted for hares and rabbits and a few from having helped thresh at harvest time. And gradually – mainly, I have to admit, at her prompting – we found things to talk about. She loved music, she said, Elvis, especially, but hadn't yet been dancing, apart from the occasional hop that was put on at the ICA Hall or the Legion of Mary; and she listened, leaning in, her expression wide with rapture, while I described what the Majorca Ballroom was like, talking as if I knew all about it, even though I'd only been there a couple of times, and keeping the focus on the bustle of the crowds and the bands I'd heard rather than the girls I'd met – not that there'd been many of those, or much of anything to confess. Finally, I helped her from the ditch and we started back, but it had been a good idea to sit a while because something had shifted between us, and we hadn't gone more than a hundred yards when she stumbled slightly against me and, under the pretence of steadying herself, slipped her right hand inside my elbow and held on, and by the time we reached Douglas again we were holding hands as if we'd been born or forged with one another in mind.

*

That was the turn I took. I can't exactly say that I put away childish things, but I could certainly feel myself growing up. Friendships remained solid enough, with Kelleher especially, because he was in the Mill with me, though in a different department, and we kicked a ball around together at lunchtimes and shared a smoke most days, but by then he'd started doing a line with Pauline Canniffe, so his time after work was also limited. It's true that there'd have been plenty of others if I had wanted them, lads to go drinking with, but I suppose there's no shame in admitting that I'd had my head turned. And it was Sally, weeks or months later, who mentioned Miss Reilly.

I'd joined her, as usual, at Chambers' Corner, at her end of the village, after putting away a hurried dinner of a few floury potatoes and a small piece of hake that must have been boiling half the day and had my jaw sore from chewing. ('No decent girl will let you near them with that breath,' Bríd had said, scowling at me across the table, though I knew by the way her canines were showing that she was thinking not of me and Sally but of whatever boy she had lined up for the evening. She hated fish, and I was glad to have arrived home to only the aftermath of her usual histrionics.) Above at the corner, not long after six, Sally took my hand and gave me her cheek to kiss, but wouldn't let me near her mouth because it wasn't yet fully dark and because women stood chatting in most of the doorways along the terrace. And in search of escape and a bit of privacy, we started over along the road towards the church.

'There's a couple from England after moving in above in Reillys,' she said, as we walked. 'He's some kind of bookkeeper, and my mother met the wife down in Bresnan's buying sausages for his breakfast and said that she's very glamorous and slow-speaking, with a big round north-country accent and her hair done up short in a way that doesn't suit her face at all. Too wide across the mouth, my mother said. But other than that, very nice. They're not staying, I don't think. They're just over to sort out her bits and pieces. He's the son, or grandson, I forget which, of a cousin.'

At first, these were just words. I listened, the way I always did whenever Sally spoke, as much for the soft tune of her voice as anything else, but the sense of what she was saying was lost on me.

'Liz Reilly,' she said, reading my blankness. 'You know.'

I nodded, but slowly. 'Is there room for them? The cousins, I mean. Or whoever they are. Those range houses are very small.'

'Sure, there's only the two of them.' She looked up into my face, studied me closely. 'You knew she died, didn't you?'

We'd planned to go as far as the Finger Post, and possibly even a bit of the way down the Passage Road, as far as Windsor, maybe, since her curfew had been relaxed a little, her father having by now taken my full measure. But there was a rawness about the evening, the weather had turned and a wind was blowing in snaps, cold in our faces and full of the smell of rain, and once we reached the church we went left and followed instead the long lane that wound between the Catholic and Protestant graveyards. We often walked the lane, and liked to, because of the towering cemetery elms and the way the road twisted, making corners that cut you off from everything and everyone; and sometimes, if it was fine and if I sensed that she'd let me, I'd press her against the old wall on the Protestant side of the road and we'd kiss, the smothering fronds of ivy working like a cushion for us against the stone. Nothing more than that, and while I tried hard to hold any devouring thoughts at bay, she kept a tight grasp of both my wrists, making sure that my hands strayed neither higher nor lower than her hips. This evening, though, because of the wind, walking had to be enough.

'I didn't know,' I said, feeling unsettled. 'And I can't understand how that could have happened. You'd think my mother would have mentioned something, or that they'd have been on about it in the Mill. Funerals are usually the talk of the place.'

'Probably they were talking about it, and your head was just somewhere else.'

She squeezed my hand, and I looked at her and, after a second, smiled.

'You were fond of her,' she said. 'It's all right to say so. I remember you carrying her bags up the hill for her. And hearing about that fight you had with Kelleher over all the slagging they used to give you. I always thought it was good of you. Because she was old and on her own.'

'I can't say why I did that,' I said. 'Most of the time she hardly even knew who I was. And she was none of my business. But I felt sorry for her. That's a fair hill up to her place, and very hard with bags of shopping.'

'They used to say she was a bit funny. My mother would sometimes pass a remark. I heard once, from your

Bríd, actually, that she'd lived with someone for a while in England. A woman, Bríd said. If you can imagine. Do you suppose that was why she never married?'

'I don't know,' I said truthfully, and flexed my hand for Sally's fingers to slip between my own. 'To me she was just an old woman. But, if I'm honest, I could sense a difference. Even if I didn't understand.'

'Poor thing, all the same. It must have been sad for her, if that's the way she was. Because that wouldn't exactly set you up for an easy life, would it?'

I shrugged. 'Life isn't easy for anyone, though. We each have our own set of problems. We're all small against the world.'

'It's difficult to imagine her young, isn't it? I wonder what she was like. Whether she was beautiful, I mean. Whether she laughed easily and a lot. Whether she was afraid of being found out, of people seeing the truth of her. Whatever that might have been.'

We'd had rain earlier in the day, and everything around us was damp. I stopped, and Sally did too, and as she turned to face me I took her into my arms. I've never been brazen, and wasn't, even then. But I felt in sudden need of an embrace, and a deep and long-held kiss.

'Love shouldn't be anybody's business,' I sighed. 'What lives between two people doesn't belong to anyone else. And maybe we don't always have to understand what it's about.'

'Love?' she asked, whispering the word as if tasting it for the first time, and I held her against me, then brought my mouth again to hers and closed my eyes.

# A Sense of Rain

I was stretched out in the centre of the bed, reading, when Ellie emerged from the en suite, naked and with her hair down around her shoulders. She stood for a moment, but then her mouth tightened and she spread a towel over the room's only chair, sat at the dresser with her back to me and began to feed the pins of the gold-and-diamond studs that I'd bought her for her last birthday into her earlobes. The right, first, and then the left.

Paris was just as we'd remembered. Our plush, well-lit hotel room was spacious – a rare enough thing in a city known for its cramped accommodations – and ideally located, overlooking the Rue du Bac and the Rue de Montalembert and with the Church of St Thomas Aquinas at our back. I'd requested a room on the fifth floor, one of the large deluxe suites with a huge king-size bed, walk-in shower and a balcony that offered views out over the city. Not quite the honeymoon suite of our first visit, five years earlier, but as much as anyone could reasonably want. An extravagance, perhaps, but one that felt justified. Because we needed Paris now in a way we hadn't then.

Since arriving on the Friday, late in the afternoon, the life we'd left behind had ceased almost immediately to exist. All the problems, all the mistakes, and almost all of the grief. That first evening, we unpacked our shared suitcase, freshened up, and ate an early dinner in the hotel restaurant, an intimate little place run by a two-star Michelin chef that seemed to have overblown its reputation only until the food arrived. By eight, we were back in the room and wrestling one another out of our clothes, as if the miscarriage, and the warnings from the doctors, was misfortune that belonged to other people. I felt light-headed and Ellie seemed possessed, and giving in to the frenzy was like coming to a banquet after a stint on hunger strike. We spoke in whispers and gasps, afraid for some ridiculous reason of being overheard, but urging one another on, helpless to stop. Yet our lovemaking, after the initial collision, had a gentle quality, too, as if we were each attuned to the other's fragility.

The door of the bathroom had slipped its clasp and fallen a couple of inches ajar, creating a sliver of white, steamy spillage, and the glow of the bedside lamp, good for an arm's reach, spilt across my chest barely enough to illuminate the pages of my book.

'Still Faulkner?' Ellie said, watching me in the mirror. I looked up from the book.

'I'm persevering. Some pages, I think I can almost understand what I'm reading.'

Her blonde hair seemed to swallow the light, and to shine. It lay in damp tendrils down her back and over her breasts, and made me think of feathers tugged loose or askew by a fighting breeze, the roadkill of field birds that have paid a bad price with traffic. Her narrow shoulders, and her long slender face and frail body reflected in the mirror, stood pallid against the dimness.

'What time is it?'

'Almost ten.'

'I'm wide awake now.'

'Good. Then come back to bed.'

She smiled. 'God, don't you ever stop?'

I was still watching her. We were watching each other, through a piece of glass, she with her back to me and with the room lying between us.

'So, get dressed,' I said. 'This is Paris. We can take a walk, stop in somewhere for a glass of wine. Or a coffee. There are places here that stay open long into the night.'

She sighed. 'My impression of Paris is always of rain. Why is that, do you suppose?'

The book lay tented open on my chest, and I picked it up, looked at the page number and tried to memorise it, knowing that without the number I'd never find my place again. And there'd be no question of me ever trying to start over. It was a slim book and I was already well into the second half, but I could only stay with it for so long. Already, my strength was waning. To avoid despair, I stopped myself from analysing or summarising what I'd so far read.

'I don't know,' I said. 'But I know what you mean.'

'When we were here last time, there was a lot of sunshine. Remember? But even then, I kept seeing the city the way it wasn't but felt as if it ought to have been. Now, it's right. Forget the songs. This is the season for Paris, I think. Rain suits the place.'

'A lot has happened here. Living and dying. Too much, maybe. That could be why.'

She leaned in closer to the mirror and used her fingertips to stretch and examine the skin beneath her eyes. 'Everything is so beautiful, the river shining with the city's lights, and all the lovers, young and old alike, strolling hand in hand or folding into one another on benches, kissing. And yet still, this sense of rain. I don't know. Even Montmartre had a melancholy, if you let yourself feel it. The artists, the light coming through the trees, a feeling of music. But that sadness too, underneath. That's what I remember.'

'Don't think about it.'

'Easy to say.'

I tossed the book down on the bed, with a piece of paper, the stub of our flight's boarding pass, tucked among the pages.

'Come on,' I said, sitting up. 'We'll go for a walk and find ourselves a nice cafe, and tomorrow we'll try the Orangerie. You said you wanted to see the Modiglianis. Then, even if it rains, it won't matter.'

She turned her head and I could see both sides of her profile, her left side – her best side, she often said – reflected in the mirror. She was looking in the direction of the door, but not at it, at something further away. The light from the bathroom was in her face now, and turned her eyes to glass. She seemed about to cry, but I waited and no tears came, and when I felt certain that that wouldn't change I stood, slipped on and buttoned a clean blue shirt, working my way slowly upwards, stepped into the same day's pair of chinos, then sat down on the bed again to tie my shoelaces.

After a minute or two, she got up and came to the side of the bed, where her clothes were laid out. Standing alongside me, close enough to touch, she too began to dress. I tried not to stare. When she leaned over, her breasts hung with exaggerated heft, and when she adjusted the elastic of her underwear between her legs I nearly reached out for her. Even all these months on, there was a slight bloat still to the flesh around the low part of her stomach, and the skin there had coarsened to an almost grainy texture.

'The museum doesn't matter,' she said, her voice all air. 'The paintings don't matter. I'll look for them, if there's time. But there's a building in Montparnasse that I'd like to visit, if we could. If we can find it. The face in a lot of Modigliani's work is that of a woman named Jeanne Hebuterne. I've been reading about him, and about her. She was his model, his muse, and his lover, too, the mother of his only child. They'd planned to marry, but her family objected to the match. It's really an awfully sad story. Modigliani was a junkie and an alcoholic, and nearly twice her age. She also painted, but didn't have what he had. She understood his genius, in a way few others did. At the time, anyway. Now, of course, we can all see, but she saw when it counted. And she adored him. Life is always hard, isn't it? No matter what you get, there's always some precious piece either missing or soon to be taken away.'

'We can go there,' I said, seeing how serious she'd become. 'Of course we can. I'll get directions at the desk. What was it? Their home?'

Ellie shook her head, half turned and considered her reflection in the dresser's mirror. The blouse, the golden colour of apple skin, went well with the bronze of her knee-length wool skirt. The top two buttons were still undone, leaving exposed a white wedge of chest and emphasising, around her neck, the silver chain, frail as filament, and the small featureless low-hanging cross.

'No.'

She looked around the room. Her shoes lay where she'd slipped them off, just at the bathroom door. One still upright, the other on its side. She stepped into them, and instantly lifted herself an inch and a half. I picked up my jacket, draping it across one arm, and opened the door for her. We walked down the corridor in silence except for the sound of our footsteps dull on the carpet, called for the lift and stood listening as it dragged itself up through the building, its iron cage groaning like an old sail ship close to collapse in a windless drift. After a minute or so, it reached our floor and braked with the sound of someone screaming through a gag. I pulled at the gate, stepped back to let her enter, then shut us both inside.

'His paintings in those days could be had for just a few francs,' Ellie said, not looking at me, looking forward. Beyond the gate's accordion lattice, layers of hotel rose up before us, floors and the concrete and girders lying between. 'More often than not, he traded them for food or his next fix. Just try to imagine that, imagine being that great, and no one caring. When he died, destitute, of tuberculosis, at only thirty-five, Jeanne was nine months pregnant, and distraught. Understandably. She was twenty-one. For most people, life is only beginning at that age. The following day, at her parents' apartment, in

116

Montparnasse, she stepped backwards out of a fifth-floor window.'

'Jesus.'

'I know. Makes you want to cry, doesn't it? How far gone does a person's mind need to be for something like that to happen? How deep does that kind of hopelessness go?'

In the lobby, a white-haired man in a fine slate-grey suit stood slump-shouldered with two suitcases in the middle of the floor while, alongside, a beautiful young girl – his granddaughter or, this being Paris, as likely as not his lover – maybe eighteen and a little too profes- sionally made up, held a phone to her ear, not speaking but smiling to herself. I followed Ellie past, nodded good evening to the smile of the hotel receptionist's *bonsoir, monsieur*, and stepped out behind my wife into the night.

The rain had stopped, but its threat had not abated, and the Rue de Beaune was quiet except for a few slow- moving cars. I took her hand and we followed the traffic the short distance to the Seine. Silence overtook us, and to fill the emptiness we set to walking, keeping to the riverside, until Notre-Dame came up ahead of us, immense in its isolation. We stopped, leaned against the wall. Somewhere in the darkness, a violin was playing. I listened and thought I recognised a Bach sonata, and then some- thing that might have been Rimsky-Korsakov.

I bowed my head. My throat had begun to ache. 'Why did you have to tell me all that?' I said, when I could.

Ellie looked at me.

'I mean, what's the good in me knowing?'

She shrugged. 'Good doesn't come into it. I read it, that's all. And it stuck. I haven't been able to get away from it, and I thought that maybe if I went there, if we went there together, we could just stand outside, and it'd make some sense.'

Her hand was dry and cool against mine, but still with a whisper of pulse. A small, delicate hand that I'd studied in so many quiet moments, mapping the veins, the spindles of bone that fanned beneath her papery skin, trimmed nails that I'd kissed and then let run across my chest and stomach, savouring their scrape.

'Imagine,' she said, as much to herself as to me, 'loving someone so much that there's nothing left of life once they've gone. Surely love is only supposed to ask the best of us. I read that there's no plaque, no memorial of any kind to mark what happened. Nothing to show for it. It's almost as if, by ignoring them, the facts can be rubbed out. That can't be right, can it?'

Below us, the river slopped against the paved embankment, its surface brushed with the powdery spill of the street lamps. And along the embankments, both on our side and across the water, couples were walking by in both directions, even this late and even with the cold, holding hands or with arms around one another's waists. I looked away so that Ellie wouldn't see me watching, and considered instead the lit facade of the cathedral, the Gothic slab with its bells and relics, built more than eight hundred years ago to replace an earlier cathedral that had stood on this same spot for probably as long again. Sleep would be slow in coming tonight, which meant that I'd have to be awake while she wept.

'Do you feel like a drink?' I asked.

She was staring at the water as if hypnotised, but after a moment shook her head.

'No? Me neither.' I turned back towards the road and waved down a taxi.

'What are you doing?'

'The driver will find the place for us.'

'Tonight?'

'Why not tonight, if it's what you need? Even if the taxi driver doesn't know, he can call it in, get directions. And we'll ask him to find a late-opening florist. This is Paris. You can leave a bunch of flowers, maybe say a prayer, if you think it'll help. That'll be memorial enough.'

Ellie remained by the wall until the taxi, which was stopped at a red light up ahead, just at the junction beside the Shakespeare and Company bookshop, crossed a couple of lanes with practised ease and drew up to the kerb for us. When I opened the car door for her, she came to my side and for just a second put a hand on my back, and in the frail lamplight I saw that she was crying, in a silent way. But she was smiling, too. I sat in beside her on the back seat and in a convoluted mixture of English and broken French helped her explain to the driver, a burly man with a thick grey moustache clotting most of his lower face, what we were looking for and where we needed to go.

# Wildflowers

He came up the road a little after six, a big man with a soft, lumbering gait, worn out from a day that had begun with the dawn milking. A brief but violent late-morning downpour had caught him in the fields and soaked him through, and even after several hours spent behind the tractor's wheel his shirt and jeans remained damp to the touch, and warm-smelling with the mineral tang of sweat. But because the sun had come out, hot enough for a while to scald, and settled the whole island with the burnished glow of a perfect August evening, his humour, having given way to torpor, was light and easy. Dragging at the air through a smile, he followed the road up between the head-high briar ditches bright on both sides with blooming fuchsia and honeysuckle and alive to the bother of wasps, bees and the occasional flitting greenfinch or babbler. He made the same traipse at roughly this time every day, even though his own home lay in entirely the opposite direction.

At home, if she'd already finished her day's chores, his wife would be sitting at the table beside the open window, her broad head bent over the crossword puzzles that she never seemed to finish. She'd fill in the short words with fat capital letters, then spend several minutes glaring at the rest of the clues, tapping the butt of the pen against her upper front teeth. When it eventually became clear to her that she'd reached an impasse, her way was to seek a six-letter space, preferably Down, because that for some reason appealed to her, though Across would suffice at a pinch, and with her usual slow care she'd spell out her own name, M-A-R-T-H-A. Were he to enter at such a moment, he'd invariably meet a look that seemed equal parts wonder and confusion, as if his appearance, even after thirty-one years of marriage, still held for her a stranger's surprise. She'd stare, eyes big behind the thick round lenses of her bifocals, then return her attention to the page, to set about colouring in the remaining blank squares so that, from a distance, if you happened to be colour-blind, you might assume the puzzle had been completed.

The evening had turned languid and the dead smut of earlier rain cloud lingered now only as a memory in the east. Weather for sitting out, he thought, pausing once just where the ditch on his right side broke for a four-rung gate, its iron rusted down to the maroon marrow of old blood. Weather for sipping a glass of cold beer and savouring the end part of another day well spent. He leaned on the gate's top rung, stopping not because he was out of breath, though he was, but so that he could savour the spill of the land, the misshapen fields empty except for patches of the same measly yellow grass that grew everywhere on the island at this time of year, and the dappled blue-glass stretch of the ocean. As a young man he'd thought often about the things that must lie on the other side of the horizon line, but having fished that water almost from the time he could stand up in a boat without needing to be held, the lesson time and tide had taught him was that the sea went on without end, with neither bottom nor sides. Beyond the horizon, there could only ever be more of the same. That saddened him, especially when he saw others go, friends, neighbours, neighbours' children, because their leaving caused him to remember again how he'd had his own heart taken that one time and drowned, and because he'd come to understand that there was nothing to be said, no words of warning that they'd heed. The whispering promises of the surf and the gold and silver that flecked the water's surface were a lure, tempting the curious-hearted away from solid footing, but those who took the bait would have to learn for themselves, the hard way, the way everybody did.

He continued to smile, forcing it now, until the sadness receded and the day was again sweet. On impulse, in turning away from the gate, he stooped and plucked some strands of goldenrod and red campion and, as an afterthought, a few wild roses, their white petals blushing a touch pink in places. Then, flowers in fist, he continued up the road, whistling the first airy strains of a tune he knew as 'The Minstrel Boy', to the little cottage set so neatly into a hard sweep of ground that it lay entirely hidden from view until you came within barely five paces of its front door.

'Hello?' he called, pushing his way inside without bothering to knock. The door, as always in hot weather, was ajar. After the sunshine of the hill road, the hallway, which led in from the side of the house and divided the tiny building fairly neatly in half, had a gloom that encouraged sighs. To his left, just inside the door, was an immaculately white late-edition bathroom, complete with toilet, sink and shower, that had been converted only in the early 1980s from a small box bedroom; and further along, another slightly larger bedroom, a shadowy room that across the span of some five generations had known seventeen births and probably a dozen final breaths.

'Hello?' he called again, raising his voice a little and feeling its heft out of place in the hallway. 'Are you here, at all?'

'I'm here,' an old woman's voice answered, after a couple of heartbeats, from ahead and to his right. Pitching without effort, though tinged with impatience. 'I'm still here.'

She was sitting in the armchair beside the living room's empty fireplace, and he knew at a glance that he'd woken her from sleep. He lingered within the frame of the room's doorway and felt his eyes drawn to the two small windows opposite. The light in here was soft and dull, diffused and made shadowy by the thin fleece of net curtain. 'There's a nice bit of sun out now,' he said. 'That drop of rain from earlier is after making the evening grand and clean. You should bring a chair outside for an hour. It'd do you a power of good.'

'Was it weeding, you were?'

'What? Oh, these.' He smiled at the posy of flowers still in his fist. 'I saw them on the way up and thought they'd brighten the place a bit for you. The ditches are

124

full of colour.' A chipped brown vase sat in the centre of the old mahogany folding table, full still with the last bunch of flowers he'd picked, some ten days or so ago. Late crocuses, violet and butter yellow, sprigs of bluebell, cerise and lilywhite foxglove. The bluebells were beginning to wilt, but the bouquet as a whole had yet to lose its vibrancy, and instead of replacing or thinning the older blooms he simply added the new cuts to the mix.

'Lazy man's load,' she mumbled, watching him from the fireplace.

He looked at her, then considered the new display. 'I don't know. I think they look good. The way they were born to look. You haven't a drop of beer going, I suppose?'

She flapped a dismissive hand. 'If you didn't finish what you brought up last week then there ought to be. You'd know better than I would.'

He continued to stand there, awkward with his size, in the middle of the floor, shoulders still slumped, the knuckles of one hand set in a frozen knocking gesture against the table's polished top. His expression looked stuck between thoughts.

'Well?'

'Well, what?'

'Is it waiting for me to pour it, you are? Go on. It'll be in the pantry if it's anywhere. And sure I'll take a drop too, so, if you're having it. Half a glass. Just for the taste. I've had the flavour of copper in my mouth all day. It's like I've been sucking pennies.'

He went through into the pantry, opened a cupboard in the corner and took out two of the small brown bottles from among the five that he'd tucked away the previous

Sunday. He twisted off the caps, poured half of one bottle slowly into a tilted glass, then stood watching creamy froth rise from the cloudy golden-red liquid. While the ale settled, he drained the remainder of the bottle in a couple of deep, thirsty swallows, then picked up the glass and the second uncapped bottle and returned to the living room.

The old woman had closed her eyes again. He stood a moment, then settled across from her in the other armchair. The only sound in the room was the thin stutter of the mantel clock shucking seconds, and because something about the thick, cool seep of the light let him consider her without needing to break down the defence of her own returning stare, he saw her more clearly than he had in the longest time.

'I'm not asleep,' she whispered, after a minute or two, in a voice almost too soft to catch.

'Don't worry,' he said. 'I have my beer.'

The faintest hint of a smile tipped the corners of her mouth. 'I wasn't worried in the least about that.'

Her face this past couple of years had begun caving in around the prod of bone, so that everything was becoming juts and hollows, her cheeks beneath their pointed ridges, her mouth between her chin and the long slender ridge of her nose. As long as he'd known her, she'd been thin. Hawkish, he supposed, in the eyes of those who didn't know her softness. But now it seemed as if her bones were shrinking, leaving her skin, baked to hide and cobwebbed with creases, to sag in a mournful way.

'Don't stay long. Martha will be wondering where you are.'

'Sure, she knows that if I'm not home I'm either in the fields or up here. She'll not worry.'

The old woman watched him pull a mouthful of ale from his bottle. Except for the life in her eyes, the focus, she was little more than husk. The glass of beer, still to be tasted, rested on one knee, gripped in her left hand, its colour deepened by the shadows, apart from a skin of white foam across its surface, the burnt, glassy brown of amber or old wood.

'How is she?'

'Ah, she's grand. The same, you know. It hurts her a bit to swallow, and some nights she keeps me awake with her whistling. It's the goitre, she says. Her grandmother had it.'

'Plenty of milk, then. And periwinkles, if she'll eat them. Tell her don't look further than the old cures.'

He and Martha were easy with one another. Love wasn't a word that generally entered their equation, though only because there'd been someone else, a long time ago, and he found it hard to give away again what had already been given once and broken. But then he hadn't been Martha's first choice either, and in time they'd both come to understand that love wasn't everything. During the first few years, when so much still seemed possible, they made the best of their situation. Having no illusions simplified matters. They were partners, sharing the workload, surviving together. And it was good to have someone. Over the years, they'd learned one another's ways, and had each grown comfortable with how the other filled space and effected the silence. Now, more than half a lifetime on, they rarely argued any more, and routine gave them not only balance but an identity. Sometimes, much more so during the early years of their marriage but occasionally even still, lying awake in the small hours, each of them listening to the hushed draw of the other's breathing, it was easy to give in to the thoughts that kept them lit, and lovely in such moments to take her into his arms and to let himself be guided in a way that met both their needs. The heart wants what it wants, but will often learn to settle for what it can get.

He hit the bottom of his bottle unexpectedly, and his thirst remained unquenched. There was beer left in the pantry but the room's reverie was such that it didn't feel quite right to move, and so he remained in his armchair, gripping the bottle and trying to enjoy the coolness of its glass against his calloused palm. Across from him, the old woman's eyes were slipping relentlessly shut. Every few minutes she struggled to revive herself only to be soon or quickly dragged back down under another wave of drowsiness.

'I'm sorry.' She cleared her throat, and stirred a little. 'It's this weather. It has me beat. I can't seem to keep awake.'

'You're lucky,' he said. 'I haven't slept properly in weeks. There's too much light out. And with Martha gasping for air alongside me I can only lie there, watching the window for the dawn. And I get to thinking. You know. About all kinds of things. That's the worst of it. I tell you, it makes the short nights feel very long.'

A fresh wave of sleep broke, and this time threatened to drown her. She went under and remained there, down at the bottom. In the armchair, she looked very small. Her feet, he noticed, tucked into square-toed shoes the leather colour of bog turf and with steel buckles that had years' since lost their sheen, barely reached the linoleum. Nothing moved, and he found himself leaning forward in search of some hint, however slight, that would signal the continuance of life. The way he and Martha had, taking turns, with the infant, Michael, all those years earlier. Not that it had made any difference in the end, because nights always kept a part of themselves hidden, and even if you succeeded in remaining awake there were still oceans' worth of things that got missed. He stared at the old woman, and for a while there was nothing to see but skin like tree bark and long, silky wisps of hair whitened to translucence by the spill of light from the nearest window. But then her mouth clenched and her tongue flashed across her thin lower lip.

'I dreamed of your father,' she said. 'All night long. I closed my eyes and there he was, the way he always was of a morning after getting the fire lit: in his shirt-sleeves and braces, his cheeks and chin dirty with a night's stubble. He turned on the wireless and we danced around the room, just like when we were first married. Slowly, hardly moving, I feeling small and safe in his arms, his body strong as a reef inside his clothes. I knew the whole time that it wasn't real but it was so vivid I could smell the oil of his skin, and I didn't want it to ever end. When I finally woke, I wept, because my mind had carried his voice in whispers back through into the morning with me.'

'It's just a dream. We all have them. Even ones like that.'

'I suppose. But they can leave such a mark. Honestly, I haven't been right all day.' She shook her head and, noticing the glass of beer, lifted it to her mouth and sipped. Froth clung to her lip and the tip of her nose. 'Can't you go, boy? Martha will have a crust on your dinner trying to keep it warm.'

He sighed. 'All right. I suppose I better. But sure, I'll be up along tomorrow. And Martha will give a call in the morning. Is there anything you need, at all?'

'Nothing for you to be fretting about.'

He hesitated, then stood, stepped close to her and kissed her cheek. Her skin was cool and rough, not as he remembered. 'Bye, Mam,' he whispered, against her ear.

She closed her eyes again and the smile deepened on her mouth. 'Bye, love. And don't forget to tell Martha what I said about the periwinkles. Tell her I said my boy is lucky to have the likes of her. Even if he doesn't always know it.'

Outside the evening seemed brighter than before, golden and lazily alive, clotted with birdsong. The sky now was clear of cloud from edge to edge, and the warm, mottled turquoise of a blackbird's eggs. He started back down the road. The slope made walking easy at first, but the gradual accumulation of gravity soon began to feel like a hand against his back, and wherever the stretch turned particularly steep he had to fight to keep from quickening into a run.

To his right, wherever the ditches broke or dropped below eye level, he caught sight of the sea glittering in the sunlight. The blueness made him think again of

Hannah. She'd lived on the other side of the island, the land side, and at fifteen, and for the couple of years that followed before taking the boat to the mainland, then to England and from there to who knew where, she'd never missed an opportunity to hold his hand. He remembered her hair jagged as whin, and her heavy-lidded eyes the Spanish colour of a burnt dirt that clenched shut in laughter, and for the better part of their teenage years they'd walked together, danced in fields, kissed whenever they thought no one was looking, traded hopes and secrets and made the best and most of any hidden places they could find.

She left, the way so many did, and once all hope of a return was lost, gone became the same as dead. But the ghosts lingered. The sight of the sea on a good day always made him recall her with a mixture of wonder and the old sadness, and if the bad days tended to heavily outweigh the good then there was still usually an hour, or five minutes, or a single heartbeat, during which the sun would seep into view and keep memories alive, and there was the constancy of the water, the waves pulling towards the land, to smash against the rocks and shore.

Without thinking, he dropped to his haunches and began to pluck more wildflowers. Bees scurried among the foxgloves, so he gathered whatever came to hand, harebell, columbine, cowslip, spools of honeysuckle, sweet violet. At home there'd be a dinner waiting on a plate, potatoes, cabbage, maybe a bit of mutton, and a bottle of something sweet to drink cooling in a water bucket in the shade. And Martha. On days like this, he had no appetite, though it would be nice to sit outside and wait for the light to fade. She'd wonder about the flowers, but wouldn't remark on them, except to smile, and if he kissed her she'd kiss him back, probably laughing as they came together. In another month, he'd turn fifty, and when he closed his eyes it was as if the years had meant nothing in their passing. He could tell himself, and believe, that he was who he'd always been, in one breath an old man, in the next still very much a boy, and he kept his losses close because time's barriers were soft.

# Segovia

T he temperature of the day had been her excuse, if she'd needed one, to step inside the bar. She'd come up that morning by bus from Madrid, with loose plans to stay a night or two, a sketch pad and a box of charcoals and pencils in her rucksack. Having seen only pictures of the place, of the castellated old town and the ancient, hulking aqueduct, her head was thick with a kind of fantasy as to what it would be like, but even in around the narrow granite and sandstone laneways there was no respite from a fiery July noon. The bar she chose was small but cool, at least by comparison with the streets, and she stopped a moment to let her eyes find their focus, then took up a position at the end of the counter, half sat and half stood against the first of the four high bar stools, and waited until someone in service appeared. Five minutes later, a youngish man did, dressed in a cold white shirt and navy slacks, his face and body thin as a matador's and as slow in his movements. 'Cerveza,' she said, holding an index finger unnecessarily in the air, her voice sounding all at once weary. He considered her for a moment, then nodded and poured the beer, filling a large glass to the top. After he'd set the glass down on a folded paper napkin and walked away, vanishing back through the side door from which he'd initially appeared, a white cap of froth formed on the beer and continued to expand until it spilt in relatively delicate fashion over the rim. Now that she had what she wanted, she held back, heightening the anticipation, then took the glass by its handle and drank to a slow depth.

The bar was laid out long and narrow, with windows only to the front, on either side of the open doorway that allowed the light to penetrate no more than five or six paces into the place. Fine sawdust clogged the cracks between the plain floor tiles and congealed where something had earlier been spilt. From a half-turn, she scanned the length of the room and somehow missed that she was not alone until, just as she was raising the glass to her mouth again, a man, far down in the shadows along the wall to her back, cleared his throat, and said, in a quiet voice that she could almost feel against her, '*Buenas tardes, señora.*'

She turned, but there was still little to see. Instead of answering, she smiled, not knowing if the gesture could penetrate the dimness, and lifted her glass. A newspaper rustled, and then there was an odd sense of a part of the floor bearing a footstep, not a sound exactly but a shift to some balance. She brought her attention back to the bar and, after another sip, set the glass down on the counter. There was really nothing to fear.

'*Inglés?*' he asked, moving to her right side, but not yet taking a seat. 'English?'

She shook her head, glanced across at him without committing to a turn. 'No, sorry. Irish.'

He was tall and thickset, fat probably, in better light, and middle-aged coming on for elderly, a big man with a strong, wide face and a high forehead stubbornly refusing the surrender to baldness. Steel-wire hair tufted the sides and top of his head in small clumps. 'What brings you to Segovia?' he asked, without expecting a reply, because a hand waved as if to dismiss his own words. 'This time of year, it is the sea you want. There at least you have the chance of a breeze. Here, you could boil eggs in our wells. It is too hot even to think.'

She smiled to herself, and didn't answer, but stared again at the glass in front of her. The froth that had spilt in the pouring had turned to clear wet coins on the varnished counter.

'But you have the right idea, at least,' he said, and when she looked at him again he nodded towards the beer and grinned, showing a row of small bottom teeth, with one missing just to the left of centre. 'It takes the Irish to educate us in sensible behaviour.'

He stepped between two stools in the centre of the bar and settled himself onto one, keeping a polite distance from her. 'Juan,' he called, lifting his voice. '*Dos cervezas, por favor.*' The bartender appeared in the doorway again, the same unhurried look about him as before but with something else, a certain obedience, evident now. '*Dos cervezas,*' the man repeated, and watched while the beer was drawn from the tap, carefully, this time, so that there was no spillage.

When the two fresh glasses were set on the counter, the man stood up from his bar stool and moved one of the beers across towards where she was sitting. She hadn't looked up, yet had observed everything, but now she turned a few degrees on her seat, and shrugged a slight thanks. He nodded his head, and his mouth tightened a little in lieu of words.

As soon as they were alone again, they set to drinking. The man drank deeply and without hurry, his eyes, fixed to a point behind the bar, growing more distant with their focus. She had to finish her first glass before starting in on the next, but that was no hardship because her thirst was wide.

'I need to leave soon,' she said, after a while. The surrounding silence, and perhaps the beer, reduced her voice to almost nothing. In this climate the alcohol settled with quick heft. 'I still need to find a place to stay.'

The man looked at her and nodded again, so she knew that he was listening. He might have recommended somewhere, and the fact that he didn't made him hard to read. He had already gone halfway down his glass and she'd yet to touch her second.

'It won't be so bad further north,' she added. 'But this is worse than I'd expected.'

'You could boil eggs in our wells, it's that hot. Did I already say? Well, it's true. Or almost. Are you going north? Get to the sea. That's my advice.'

'I am thinking about Bilbao. In a few days. But I also want to visit Burgos. There are cave paintings. That interests me. Have you seen them?'

'No. I've been to Burgos many times, but not for some years now, and never to visit caves.'

'I paint. Not seriously, I don't mean seriously. But it's just something I like to do. And, in fact, it's why I'm here. I want to draw the castle.'

'Many come for that purpose, yes. It's famous. They say it's the castle that inspired Walt Disney, the one that opens his cartoons. Perhaps that is true, perhaps not. And perhaps it doesn't even matter as long as people think it's true. But there are better things to see in Segovia than rocks and rooftops.'

'That depends. We all have different needs.' She could feel herself speaking slowly, but whether because of the shadows or the beer she didn't know.

'And you need fairy tales, is that it?'

She looked at him and felt, all at once, the press of tears. But he hadn't meant to challenge her, and his voice was soft, thickened by whispers, as if he had been too long around sick people. She finished her first glass with a last long swallow, then manoeuvred the second into place between her resting hands.

'Of course I do,' she said. 'Who doesn't, at my age?'

'What are you talking about? You're what? Early thirties?'

'I'll be forty-two next month.'

'Well, still. So what? That's no age. You're a beautiful-looking woman, a flower in bloom. And you've got a whole long life ahead of you. Take it from an old fool who knows too well what he's talking about, and be grateful for that.'

'Of course.' She glanced at him again, in a small way, and lifted her glass to her lips. The man was right; she had a kind of beauty. Men had always looked, and always thought so.

Hair the sand-blonde of old hay styled short but full and carelessly loose, with the finger-combed fringe that suggested at once coyness and daring, a small mouth, slender nose and morose eyes the dirty blueness of a daytime just ahead of storm. Since girlhood, she had been a draw for those who cared to look closely, and she'd always made the most of her appeal. But this heat discouraged the facade of make-up.

'I am actually a stranger here myself,' he said. 'I was born in Ávila. It's not even an hour away now by car but, back then, miles had more distance about them. I lived for a while in Salamanca and a while longer, after the army, in Madrid, thinking that I needed to be in a big city, one of those places where I could live and be lost at the same time, if I was ever to make anything of myself. It was in Madrid that I started to learn English.'

'You speak it wonderfully.'

'Evening classes. And since then, from books. Hemingway, Chandler. The English writer, Graham Greene. Women, too, occasionally. After more than forty years, I am still learning.'

'So what brings you to Segovia?'

'Oh, the same as you. Fairy tales.' He showed her his teeth again, a grin so comfortable in its place that his face should have looked emptier without it. But this was not so. She sensed that he would have been equally himself in any expression. It was one of the things age gave to a certain type of man. 'I followed a woman here. A girl, really. Isn't that the best reason to do anything? Of course,

I don't mean yesterday or last week. I was twenty-five, she was seventeen. Forty-two years ago now. 1974. She'd snared me in Madrid, at the cafe where she had found summer work and where I went every single day after first seeing her there. By September, I had a choice to make: to either come here after her or lose her entirely from my life. But we were already lovers by then, so it wasn't really much of a choice at all. And she knew how weak I was for her.'

'That's a nice story.' She drank again from the glass. The beer dug cold channels into her, yet didn't seem to touch her thirst. The void that had defined her these past few months was swallowing everything. 'I hope it ended happily ever after for you both.'

The old man shrugged. 'Ever after is asking too much. Can a life without its downs as well as ups count as fully lived? I don't know. But yes, we were happy, I think. If I am forced to answer, I will say so. Maria was a good woman and an even better wife. She's been dead four years, and I still wake every morning expecting to find her beside me in our bed. Being with someone at first is like a slow dance. You are conscious of every moment, and of taking a wrong step. For years, when you're alone, you are the person you think yourself to be. But love changes everything. You come to understand, though not always in words, that the other person makes you complete. Maybe it is because you have given away your heart. And once you've grown used to having them there, so close, their absence opens a hole that can never again be filled. You have to go on, of course, but you never quite regain your balance.'

He let his words tremble into laughter. 'Sorry,' he said, and he started to reach out towards her, but settled for putting his right hand palm down on the hard red leather seat of the stool that stood empty between them. 'It's this heat. Time feels as if it's stopped. And I get maudlin on beer. Just ignore me. Please. I am alive today, and that makes me one of the lucky ones. I get to walk in the sun, I get to sit in a bar and think my thoughts. And today, at least, I get to chat with a beautiful young woman and maybe, if she will let me, to buy her another drink.'

'I've barely touched this one,' she said. 'And two is already over my limit. I'm not really supposed to drink at all.'

'Well, what does it matter? One more won't make a difference now.'

'I still need to find a hotel or a guest house. If I'm going to stay, I mean.' She closed her eyes, and exhaustion was right there. 'All right. Just one more. For the road.'

'Juan,' the man called, not raising his voice but speaking with a different kind of assurance.

When the young bartender reappeared he didn't wait for instructions but set about pouring two more beers. She watched him work, his slow, measured movements announcing a tensile hardness, the lines of his strong young body inside the shirt, the narrow back and waist. Again she thought of a matador, how she imagined one might be based on some of the pictures she must have seen in books. He was handsome, especially in profile. Chiselled for an audience or a movie screen. She wondered if there was an age when a person stopped being their mother's child and became entirely themselves, if the growing apart was not only natural but inevitable, even essential.

'Are you in pain?'

She hadn't even realised that she was holding her stomach with both hands, or that her face had drawn itself into a wince. The old man had got up from his seat and was standing at her side, one hand easy across her shoulders in a kind of protective half-embrace. For a second she yearned for that, for the feeling of having somebody close. She tried to smile. 'It's nothing. Cramps, that's all. The coldness of the beer on an empty stomach. Really, I'm fine. But perhaps I'll leave this beer, if you don't mind. And I'd better be going.'

Juan stood behind the counter, watching. If he was concerned, or cared at all, then it didn't show. But the old man's expression was full of worry. He stepped back in order to let her up from her seat, but the arm that had been on her shoulders remained outstretched, hanging in the air and ready to catch her if she stumbled. She felt conscious of her movements now, but the sensation in her stomach – not cramps at all, but a memory of something worse – remained with her, causing her to react slowly and in an exaggerated fashion. She straightened the skirt of her dress, cotton flower-patterned pleats, down over her thighs, then stooped for the rucksack that she'd dropped at the foot of her bar stool.

'Let me take that for you,' the old man said, reaching for the backpack, but she drew it against her chest.

'No, it's fine. It's nothing. I can manage on my own.'

He hesitated. 'Then let me at least walk with you and help you choose a place. We'll find somewhere to fit whatever budget you have. If they see that you are with me you'll be sure to get a better price.'

'I thought you said you were a stranger in these parts.'

'I am. Unless you belong ten generations to Segovia, you're a stranger. It's the same here as in any small town. But forty years still counts for something. I have a business here. People know me. That helps.'

'What sort of business?' She considered him again, still with the rucksack cradled tightly in her bare arms. She saw him staring at her forearms and wrists, the skin smooth and tanned to old gold over bones that gave an impression of fragility – not, she knew, in an altogether unattractive way – and for those few seconds his vigour seemed to belie his age. Nothing else about him had changed, except that a lightness had come into his eyes, and she understood that there was more to him as a man than she'd already seen.

'This place,' he said, and opened one arm, palm splayed. 'This bar. I've been running it for more than half my life. Sometimes I have no idea at all where the years went. Juan runs it now, but I still like to be around. It is important to feel as if we matter, even when we no longer do.'

She looked at him, then lowered her backpack to her side and moved towards the door. He read her slow pace as an invitation to follow. Outside, away from the doorway, the brightness of the day was blinding. She hadn't realised how cool the bar had been or how good and refreshing the beer had tasted. Within seconds of having moved between the two atmospheres, perspiration began to blister her temples. Buildings converged, the streets narrowing and heightening to a claustrophobic sepia, and the ground, lined in ancient, broken cobble, put up a severe challenge even to her low-heeled sandals. She saw him watching where she walked, the flesh around his eyes etched in dread that the least misstep would cause a twisted or even broken ankle, and her gratitude for his concern was genuinely felt even as it ebbed back into sadness. She had a pair of good shoes in her rucksack, bought on a whim back in Madrid with the vague idea of perhaps dressing up some night for dinner in one of the city's nice restaurants, but indolence and the awareness of her isolation had kept that from happening.

'I know a nice hotel near here,' he said, after they'd been walking for a couple of minutes. 'With rooms starting at about forty euros. Is that too expensive? If it is, I can find you somewhere else, but this one is attached to a cafe that serves very good tapas, and they know me there because it's a place I often come to eat. I'll speak to the manager on your behalf and try to strike the best deal. I think you will find nothing better for the price unless you can sacrifice your central location.'

'No, that sounds fine,' she said, though it was more than she'd expected to have to pay. She'd been on the road three weeks, trawling in slow fashion for the sake of her savings, from Malaga and Granada in the south, up through Seville, Cordoba and Toledo. In Madrid she had managed to find a half-decent room for thirty a night and was expecting Segovia to cost her even less than that. A hostel would have sufficed. She glanced at him and wondered if he noticed how brittle her voice had become. Again, she felt the ache to cry, but resisted giving in, having already cried too much for all the things she could not change.

A bend in the street smothered the sunlight, leaving them in shade as dense as windowless rooms. Then the buildings separated again and the light returned in a searing way, obliterating detail. She stopped and raised a hand to shield her eyes, instantly if momentarily blind.

'Are you sure you're okay?' He reached for her rucksack and this time she let him take it. She nodded that she was, that it had already been a long day for her and she was just tired now but would be fine once she could lie down.

By six, she had spread a large bath towel across the seat of the room's single armchair, a low wing-back, upholstered in faded paisley, and settled herself just inside the open, curtained window. Stillness filled the afternoons with disquiet, their suffocating blaze lengthening interminably the sense of solitude. But once the light began to wane and in its cooling shifted towards something resembling a breeze, being alone felt bearable. And wasn't that the same, surely, as giving up, surrendering to your lot? Refreshed and still naked from the shower, she leaned back in the towel-covered chair and her hand went to her stomach again and turned a slow backwards circle, then rose up and loosely cradled her right breast. Having lost what little substance she'd had, she felt hollowed out. At forty-two, even her fantasies had slipped away.

He'd been kind. They talked about meeting later, for dinner, and when she seemed reluctant he said that he'd come anyway, because he had to eat, and that if she felt like it, if she'd slept or rested enough, she could still choose to join him. He hoped to see her, he said, just before opening the door; he would be very glad of her company. And the food here was worth trying because it would give her a true flavour of the place. She had sat on her side of the bed, not looking at him, looking at the floor, the bare varnished boards made of old wood knitted together, and said that she might be down if, as he said, she could get some sleep, but that he should not expect her, and that he shouldn't wait, or read anything into it if she didn't appear. He wouldn't, he said, holding on to a dignity that no longer much mattered, but he'd be there from about nine o'clock onwards, either in the cafe or in the hotel's bar, and he'd continue to hope.

Beyond the white web of the curtains, lazy rush-hour cars hummed and rumbled past, and the first twinge of dusk had bruised the latening hour.

Some of his questions, she'd answered, but in halves. There was a right time to ask them, after the walls had come down, as long as he was careful about cutting too deep. He'd opened the window but had left the curtain drawn, the light gauze, which helped diffuse the light, so that being awake no longer felt quite so painful.

'Did you ever marry?' he asked, from somewhere very close, and she opened her eyes without realising that she'd shut them, looked at him for a second or two, then shook her head. 'No,' she said, and fought an urge to bite her lip, an old habit that she'd never fully given up. 'That is to say, not officially. Not in the eyes of church, or any god. But sort of, I suppose, once, for a while. For almost five years, if you could be less than literal about the facts of it.' What her mother and those of that generation and before would have called living in sin. Because David – his name was David – had already been down the aisle, marriage wasn't on the cards. He referred to her as his partner, and introduced her as such whenever the situation required it of him, so it had become the accepted term for what they had going. But that word also implied equality, evenly split shares in everything and backs to the wall together, and the reality was that she'd never been cut out for living in such a way. Her flesh was one thing, but the essential parts of herself, those that made her who she truly was, could only ever belong to her alone.

'Children?'

'Why?'

'What do you mean?'

'Nothing.' She hesitated. 'Don't ask everything of me. I'm not a book for you. I'm not a story. Don't ask for everything.'

'If I was doing that, I apologise. I don't want to upset you. That's the last thing I'd want.'

'You haven't. I'm not. No. No children. To answer your question. I'm alone.'

At first he said nothing. Then he cleared his throat. 'It was just something to say when you hope to get to know someone better, that's all. A way of trying to understand who they are.'

'That's asking an awful lot.'

'I didn't mean for it to be.'

'I know, but the next question would have been about what I do, how I make a living. Then about where I was born and grew up, where I went to school. Or my parents,

and brothers and sisters. People are more than these defin-
itions. You're looking in the wrong place, if you are hoping
to see who someone really is.'

The light in fading felt as thick and slow as honey
coming off a spoon and, haunted by the sensibilities of
sleep, made for burdened movements. She let the air come
into her and through her, and watched the waxy yellow-
greyness turn dirty where it seemed to bunch against
the horizon line. Wings of shadow spilt from the buildings all the way down the left side of the street, and as
pleasing as the view happened to be she found herself
wishing for a sight of the aqueduct, for the way it would
surely shape and hold its shade at this hour and for
how even the dying light would flare in gluts through
its archways. In terms of the things they built, the Romans
were forever. These great constructions were their veins
and muscles, these aqueducts, roads, statues and amphi-
theatres, their flesh and blood and bones. And maybe,
too, their idea of a heaven worth achieving. Yet it was
also all just stone. Grand, beautiful, ingenious and built
to last, but still, ultimately, nothing more than the boast
above the grave, markers commemorating those otherwise
forgotten. Eventually, all rivers run dry.

She liked being naked in this chair, and to have the
opened window ahead of her, as if she were offering herself
up to the city's embrace. But the reality wasn't that at all,
because the curtain, and the two floors of elevation, and
behind her, the empty room with its locked door, helped
keep her hidden. The bed was tossed, the top blankets
pulled or kicked away, the sheet damp from sweat. She
sat a moment longer, then went and lay down, and when

the sight of the ceiling became too much, she threw a forearm across her eyes and stretched out until her hips lifted and her legs thrashed apart. And at last, after enough time had gone by, she got up again and began to dress.

At the bottom of her rucksack, in a clear plastic bag, was her last clean dress, the crimson flash. She slipped on her underwear, changed her mind and decided to forgo the bra, just for tonight, and stepped into the dress, stretching it into place around her waist, rump and breasts. Then she straightened the string-tied shoulder straps, let her fingertips trace the neckline's plunge all the way to the dead centre of her chest, and stooping a little to make the best use of the room's mirror, began, almost without thought, to tidy the mess of her hair.

He'd been nice to her. He had kind eyes, big gentle hands, shoulders that could put a wall between her and everything else, if that was what she needed. She'd leave it until nine or half past before going down, and she'd eat and let herself be fed. That gave her a couple of hours. Feeling both lost and at home, she returned to the bedside and stood rummaging through the rucksack until she found her good shoes, the ones she'd not yet worn.

# The Aftermath

The woman enters first, through the double-bolted door into a third-floor room bare except for a standing lamp in one corner and, against the far wall, a wooden pallet serving as a bed and on top, heaped as they had been abandoned, a sleeping bag, a large pink quilted blanket and a soiled pillow. Beside the lamp, on the floor, is an olive-green plastic electric kettle plugged into a nearby socket, and two dirty white mugs.

Seconds behind her, the man appears in the doorway. He is wearing a fawn trench coat, worn open, over an unremarkable grey suit, and his tie hangs like the tongue of something monstrous from his coat pocket.

'Well? Are you coming in, or not?'

'What? Oh, yeah.'

He steps into the room, closes the door, and leans back against it.

'There's coffee, as long as you don't need milk or sugar.'

'Fine. Thanks.'

She moves past him, coming intentionally close. Her clothes have the tiredness of stage costumes: high heels, tan leather jacket that looks a size too small and which she wears with the sleeves pushed up her long forearms and, underneath, a yellow T-shirt that only reaches to the waistband of her short denim skirt. She glances around as if looking for something, then slips the strap of her handbag from her shoulder and sets it down on the floor.

'Come in,' she says again. He nods his head but doesn't yet move.

In front of him, bending from the waist in a way that with her legs straight and slightly apart is surely meant to tease, she picks up the mugs, throws the slops and dregs out carelessly onto the floor, pours a little water from the kettle into each, repeats the process, and switches on the kettle to boil.

When she turns back to face him again, she catches him staring. He lowers his eyes, not necessarily out of embarrassment. There is a look of memory on his face. She hands him the mugs, and he holds them while she fumbles in her jacket pocket for a couple of sachets of instant coffee, tears them open and shakes one into each. Then she takes the mugs back from him and sets them again beside the kettle.

'Should we take off our coats?'

In answer, the man slips off his trench coat, folds it carefully lengthwise, and brushes away some real or imagined dirt. The woman peels off her own jacket, then accepts his coat, balls them up together and throws them down onto the floor at the foot of the sleeping bag. The man watches, but doesn't speak.

'That's better. Don't you think that's much better? Now we can get comfortable.'

Her T-shirt is sleeveless, with armholes large enough to reveal clear glimpses of a white lace bra. She glances at him in a covert way, then stretches, raising her arms high above her head, exposing two or three inches of her stomach.

'I like these hours. The day catches up on you. Don't you find that? But it's good to be able to kick back and relax. These couple of hours before sleep have a kind of calm that I like.'

He is listening and nods, yet seems distracted.

'I can't stretch like that any more,' he says. 'Not since I put my back out that time. They've all looked, doctors, chiropractors, even acupuncturists. But no one knows anything about backs. I mean, not really. I've read that swimming is good for it, for an injury like that. But I can't swim. Never learned.'

'Well, don't worry. I won't make you stretch. Or swim either. Not if you don't want to. I can stretch enough for both of us.'

The room is squalid, with torn, shabby orange-and-brown wallpaper on the walls, a window partly concealed by a bath towel being used as a makeshift curtain. The air in here has a gritty staleness that he can feel between his teeth.

'I know,' she says, reading him. 'The place could definitely do with a lick of paint.'

'A lick?'

'Well. Money's hard to come by. You should know that as well as anyone. We're not all lucky, you know. And you get what you pay for.'

'I know, sorry. I didn't mean anything by it.'

'I'll make the coffee. If you want, you can sit down.'

The man looks at her, then, following the dart of her stare, at the pallet and its crumpled sleeping bag. He nods, moves to the makeshift bed and lowers himself in an awkward, careful way, then slumps back against the wall. Across the room, the woman drops into an easy squat, and pours boiling water into each mug. In that position, she has her back to him. Her tabby hair spills in bundled crescents down between her shoulder blades, and her short skirt rides a long way up her thighs. After a few seconds, she stands again and crosses the room to the sleeping bag, carrying the two mugs.

She holds out a mug for him to take. 'I hope you're okay with instant.'

'Instant's fine. Thank you. Anyway, it's all I'm used to.'

'I often think that if I ever come into money, the first thing I'll buy is a decent coffee machine. And from then on, I'll only ever drink the real stuff.' She sits down alongside him on the pallet, keeping just apart so that the lengths of their bodies are almost but not quite touching. 'And the second thing I'll buy is a bed.'

The man sips his coffee, and winces because of the heat. Her arm alongside his own is propped up on a raised knee, her skin the colour of pine, her hand bent slack at the wrist, the gesture despite everything beautiful as a slow dance.

'But then,' he says, 'after that, you'll want chairs, then a table, new wallpaper, carpet maybe, a radio, a television. And you'll find that none of it is that much of an improvement on instant.'

She stiffens. 'I might not find that. And I'll probably sleep a whole lot better. At least then I won't have to worry so much about cockroaches. That's why I have the pallet. To stop them crawling into the sleeping bag. No wonder I have nightmares.'

'Does the pallet stop them?'

'No. But I think it helps. It raises me up a few inches. It's not much, and it's no guarantee, but it makes some difference.' She looks at him until he meets her eye. 'Do you find it warm in here?'

'Warm? No, not especially. It's not cold, but I wouldn't say warm.'

'I find it warm.' She sets her mug of coffee down on the floor, then in a single smooth and clearly practised motion, crosses her arms and peels off her T-shirt. 'There. That's much better.'

He studies the side of her face, illuminated in the lamplight, until his eyes are drawn to her body. But after a moment, he catches himself and looks away. He tastes the coffee, and seems to want to say something but thinks better of it and hides his mouth on the mug's rim.

'Are you hungry?' she says, after a few seconds have passed.

He shakes his head. 'I'm fine.'

'I'm starving. I wish I'd thought to eat today. I don't know what it is, what's the matter with me, but lately I've been forgetting things. I'll be thirty-three in a month. When you put it into numbers, it doesn't seem like much. But it's as if my mind has become too full. Can that actually happen, do you think? Maybe there are things I need to forget, just to free up some space. I find myself slowing down, the way computers do when they've been used too much and for too long. I've eaten nothing since yesterday. And some days, I don't think I even notice. Coffee's the problem. Drinking coffee always gives me an appetite.'

'If you want, later on, I mean, we could go out for something. A burger, a sandwich, something like that.'

'I'd like that,' she says, then clears her throat and coughs lightly.

'Sure. Good.' Then, abruptly, he stops speaking, leans forward a few inches from the wall and strains to listen. 'What's that?'

'What?'

'Listen.' He looks at her. 'That. Do you hear it?'

She leans forward, too, her head slightly inclined. 'What? Cars?'

'No. Not cars. Not traffic. I don't hear it now. It sounded like …'

'Like what?'

'I don't know. Like crying, I think. Sobbing. Very quiet. Like a child sobbing. Quiet and far away.'

'Oh. One of the neighbours, I expect. A television. I'm the only tenant on this floor, but a few of the rooms on the floor below are let out, and there are always noises. Or else it's just the pipes. Sound carries, you know. And this is an old house, and the plumbing's not worth the shit that clogs it. You'd want to hear it late at night. When everyone's asleep. Cries for hours, sometimes. If houses can cry then this one takes the top prize. Everyone knows not to flush after eleven, but I don't think it makes much of a difference.'

The man is still listening. 'I don't hear it now.'

'No.'

The woman, apparently out of boredom, kicks off her shoes. Cerise-pink leather slip-ons with slim four-inch heels, they clatter across the floor, first one and then the other. The man watches them, then stares at her feet. She notices.

'I have nice feet, don't I?'

'What?'

'My feet. Don't worry. It's okay to look. I don't mind. Some women have ugly feet. Even beautiful women.'

'Yes.'

'But I have nice feet. Don't you think?'

The man looks, and nods his head slowly. 'Fine, yes.'

She smiles at something from another time and place, then runs her hand up the slow length of her thigh, bringing with it, beneath the flat of her palm, her skirt's hem. He can't look away. Her flesh, in the lamplight, has a buttery sheen.

'So,' she says. 'What would you like to talk about?'

He shrugs. 'Anything. I don't know. It's not important what we say.'

'I'm not really thirty-three.'

He looks up at her.

'I'm actually thirty-six. Or thirty-seven. What year is this again? I was born in 19 ... well, it doesn't matter. Let's pretend it doesn't matter. Thirty-six or thirty-seven. Not much in it. I don't even know why I said I was thirty-three. Just like I don't know why I'm saying all this now.' She breaks into silence, but everything is tight behind the press of more to come. He watches her and she looks back at him. Then she clears her throat again, very gently. 'Do you know me?'

He hesitates. 'I don't know. I know someone like you. Or, I did. Once upon a time.'

'A woman?'

'Yes.'

'Your wife?'

'Not any more.'

His gaze drifts across the floor again. One of the shoes, the left one, has settled on its side, its cavity gaping towards him. The other has managed to land upright, and lifted by its heel seems to tower above its companion. A pair still, but somehow no longer compatible.

'Tell me about her. Describe her to me. Did she have long hair? Green eyes? Did she whisper things to you in bed? Tell me,' she says, reaching out, taking his hand and laying it, very gently, on her bare thigh. 'Did she feel like this?'

As if in reflex his fingers spread and his hand shifts and settles of its own accord a comfortable and more compelling half an inch higher. He sighs. 'She looked like you. Yes.'

For several seconds more they remain this way, the man staring at his own hand high up on the woman's thigh, his little finger touching, resting against, but not pressing, the still-hidden lace of her panties, the woman looking with a kind of wonder at the side of his face. With neither of them having moved perceptibly, they've drawn very close, and he can feel her slow exhalations against his cheek and the skin beneath his ear. Then he turns and meets her eyes, and as if there is nothing else for them to do they bow to one another in a kiss.

*

'Nick?'

He is sitting in a small, clean office dominated by wood, the large mahogany desk in front of a window made dusky by three-quarters-drawn venetian blinds, the walls cloaked corner to corner in shelves of leather-bound books. There is enough light to see, though not to scour, and its source is not immediately apparent. Across a short empty span of timber floor, a frail-looking man, elderly, sits on a straight-backed chair, his legs crossed tightly at the knee and his hands twisted together in a prayerful grip. A therapist with almost thirty years' experience, retired now apart from the few cases that continue to interest him. Nick registers the cap of white hair and the equally white, meticulously shorn beard, and also the blue-grey suit worn in a casual way, without its tie and with the throat buttons undone.

'Nick?'

He lifts himself a little, as if coming to, straightening his posture in the leather bucket chair that seems to have been specifically designed for slouching.

'Yes, sorry. I wish I could answer. That's what I wish for more than anything. But it's so hard to say.'

'How often are you seeing her now?'

'Twice a week. I'd like it to be more, and there are times, when we're together, that I never want to leave.'

'But?'

He closes his eyes. 'Don't make me say it.'

'I won't,' the older man says. 'But, Nick, if you ever really hope to get past this, sooner or later you're going to have to.'

The seconds gather and turn awkward. An unseen clock is ticking in jerks. Nick glances towards the door and, keeping his eyes averted, clears his throat.

'It's a relief to go. To be able to just get up and walk away. To abandon her. Is that what you want to hear?'

'It's not a question of what I want.'

'Every time I go to her, I set myself on staying. And still, the moment comes when I just can't be around her. I despise myself for pulling back. Because she needs me, even if she doesn't know it.'

'We've talked about this. The way you feel is natural, this need to be there for her and at the same time wanting to just run and hide. It's nothing to be ashamed of. But it is confusing, and acknowledging that much is an important step. The problem is that, when it comes to extreme trauma, the aftermath is unpredictable. It's not an exact science. Everybody responds differently and heals at his or her own pace. You can't expect too much at once.'

Nick clenches a tissue in one fist. There's always a box ready, in case he needs to cry, but tears only tend to come at smaller hours, spilling out from the corners of his eyes when he is lying alone in his big double bed, when the walls built to separate years' worth of memories crumble in on one another, bringing forgotten moments leaping back to life.

'She has no past,' he says, talking as much to himself as to the old man. 'Her mind has built this new reality. And it's her act that's the hardest to take.'

'What do you mean?'

'This prostitute business. It's as if the thought of me throws a switch in her head. I know that as soon as I'm out the door the front comes down. For a while I struggled with that, but I've watched her, just to make sure. And I've had her watched. There's no one else. But when she sees me, she becomes this, I don't know what to call it. This other person. She even dresses the part, and turns hard, cruel, in a way she's never been.'

'She needs a shield,' the doctor says. 'It's actually less surprising than you might think. A part of her craves you, craves the intimacy, and her mind has to deal with that, and to punish her for such wants. It's guilt, fear, shame. She's doing it because she needs to suffer.'

'What gets me most is that she knows me. I'm sure of it. Twice a week, either when I come to her place or when we meet somewhere, she smiles at the sight of me. For a second I get a glimpse of how she used to be. She lights up, but as quickly as it happens, it's gone. She kisses my cheek, but she has never spoken my name. Not once. Not since, well ...'

Again, the silence, and underneath, the clock, ticking.

'Go on.'

'That's one of the things I long for now. Stupid, I know. You wouldn't think it'd be that big a deal. But just to hear my name in her voice would mean something. Whenever I ask her, though, she looks away. We make love, and I try to believe that will awaken something. I keep hoping it will. In the dark, that close, that connected, it feels the same as always. But it feels different, too. Sometimes, after we've finished, she cries. Sometimes, in the middle of everything, she turns her face away from me. She seems to be able to surround herself with silence. Like a shell. And no matter how hard I beat at it, it won't crack. I've begged her, I've shouted at her. But she doesn't even seem to hear me. It's like her body is reacting to me, but the rest of her, the part of her that matters most, is far away.'

The older man's expression is difficult to read, caught in some tight neutrality, but there's a hint of softness evident.

'And there's something else,' Nick says. 'I don't know how to explain this, but I never use her name either. It's not that I don't want to, because I do, all the time, but it won't come out of me. It seems that I'm holding back, too.'

'And now?'

'Now, what?'

'How about saying it now. Her name. Here. For me.'

Nick just stares at him.

'Even if you can't say it to her, it might do you good to get it said.'

'You don't understand.'

'What, Nick? What don't I understand? Tell me what I'm missing.'

'Her name's not the issue. It's the gulf that's opened up between us. I can say her name, just not to her.'

'So, say it now. For me.'

The bones of his jaw feel tight. He sits motionless in the chair but looks ready to tear the room apart, to kick holes in the wall.

'Lucy.' His lips move but there is no sound at all.

The older man leans forward.

Nick clears his throat. 'Lucy,' he repeats, with more force. 'There. You happy now?'

'That's good, Nick. You might not think it, but it matters.'

'No it doesn't. Let's not fool ourselves.'

'Give it some time,' the therapist says. 'Small steps. But you have to understand that your marriage will either get better or it won't. You may need to check your expect-ations. I know it's hard to hear but what's past really might be gone. And sometimes, what we have now is what there is. What's most important is your recovery. Yours and Lucy's. The question you have to ask yourself is, can that be enough for you? You can hope for more, even pray for it, if that helps you. But don't assume that it'll work out. Because you can't. The truth is, nobody knows. Not the doctors, not me, not a priest.'

The tissue in Nick's fist is turning damp. He wants to close his eyes, or lower them to something easier, but it's as if they need the sting of pain.

'I sometimes think that if I could only sit her down and talk about it, I'd make her understand. If she could just look at me the way she used to, and not be afraid to let me see her, I'd happily deal with the rest.'

The therapist removes his spectacles, finds a handker-chief in his jacket pocket and begins to carefully wipe the lens. 'In an ideal world, a frank conversation would help you both,' he says finally. 'You'd sit and talk and in that way begin to heal. But if that were to happen, if Lucy could ever be honest with herself about it all, she may not respond as you hope. The shock to her system could be immense, and that's something you'd need to prepare for. At the moment, she's hiding. You think you're not, and that you're okay, but you've bottled an awful lot up yourself. Even here, to me, you'll admit to certain things, mistakes, but you keep them at a remove. That's all right, that's how we survive. But you'll feel it, when the skin starts to come off. You blame yourself for what happened, but it would be very different if she started blaming you. You think you know pain, and you do, but this would take it to a new height. And there's no guarantee you'd find that easy to bear.'

Nick leans forward and tries to think. But he's tired, almost worn out. With effort, he steels himself for what's to come.

'That doesn't matter,' he says. 'I'll take that pain, if I need to. Hers and mine, both. It's not even a choice. Because we can't go on like this.'

'No,' the therapist sighs. 'I don't suppose we can.'

'The challenge is getting her to see the world as something more, something better, than the fantasy she's built. But when I try to speak about anything important, she looks right through me. If she'd only listen, I'd tell her that none of this was down to her, that it wasn't her fault. I'm the one who had her on the road that night. We can cut it a dozen ways, but there's bones in that fact. It was me. My selfishness, my fault. I could have got a lift, or called a taxi. But no. Even if she was the one who offered, I accepted. And I didn't have to. So I'm to blame. For everything.'

'Nick.'

'No matter how far back you trace the pieces, I'm the one who put it all in motion. I'm the cause. I'm to blame. And I wish I could just tell her. I wish I could lift that from her, you know?'

'Nick, it's natural to feel that way. But believe me when I tell you it's not what she wants to hear. It's likely, in fact, that she can't hear it.'

'When I start saying it, I almost can't stop. It's like vomit. And it does me a kind of good, but afterwards all I have left is emptiness. Because they're only words. And really, it's just a thing to say. Because what do I know about it? I mean, it wasn't my head against the windscreen.' His voice begins to crumble, his breath tightening to musical notes in his throat. 'And it … wasn't me who … who, had, to, hear the …'

Nick's face collapses, and the therapist catches a glimpse of the devastation before the mess is gathered into cupped palms. He waits without speaking or moving, waiting for the tears to abate.

*

Days later the woman, Lucy, is alone on a park bench backed by a slope of grass and scattered alder saplings. It is still only April but summer has begun to show itself early, the air already thick with heat and the sky the sort of unblemished azure that encourages stasis. Ahead, a broad but shallow river bends to within twenty feet of her, and she watches it in a kind of trance.

This afternoon she has made an effort. She has on a modestly short light green cotton dress, with string-like shoulder straps that emphasise the shapeliness of her collarbones, shoulders and upper arms, and she sits with her legs snugly crossed and her right arm stretched along the top of the bench's uppermost rung. Everything is in bloom. With her hair knotted up into a casual ponytail she looks young, almost girlish. Beside her on the bench, a dog-eared paperback book lies face down on its open pages.

After some time the man, Nick, approaches from the upriver direction, but she is so engrossed by the water that she doesn't notice until he is beside her. When he reaches out and touches her shoulder she looks up, not at all startled, shielding her eyes with one hand against the sunlight. He smiles hello but she just stares. He is in his blue shirt, with the collar unbuttoned and the sleeves rolled to his elbows, and the grey jacket of his suit is draped over one forearm.

'I'm glad you came,' he says.

'You asked me to. And I said I would.'

'I know. Well, anyway. I'm glad.'

She nods, squinting against the glare of the sun, then picks up her book from the bench beside her and sets it down on her right side, a gesture he reads as an invitation to sit. For a moment it feels awkward. She hasn't shifted an inch from the centre of the bench, and while there is plenty of room for him, their positions suggest an undeniable intimacy. He lays his suit jacket over the bench's armrest, and leans back.

'This is nice,' he says, trying with his voice to express some state of relaxation that he doesn't quite feel.

'Hmm. It is.'

'And there's real heat in the day. They're saying we could be in for a good summer.' He smiles. 'Those ducks look to be enjoying themselves.'

'How do you know?'

'Well, I don't. I just mean, they look to be.'

She turns to him. 'For all you know, this is how ducks always act. For all you know, they could be in mourning. Or contemplating suicide.'

'Well, yeah. I suppose so. I mean, it's possible. Anything is possible.'

'That's not true, either. I can think of plenty of things that are not possible.'

'It's just a figure of speech.'

He sees her lips tighten and tuck in at the corners, opening dimples.

'Why are you always so placating? Your wife must hate that about you.' She considers him, her tone calm, detached. 'Seriously, do you think that's an attractive quality in a man? Do you think that's what women like? Or want? Or need?'

'I don't know,' he says. 'I haven't thought about it. I don't do it for those reasons. I don't do it for any reason. It's just who I am. I want to be supportive.'

'And you think a few inane words about ducks, or peddling your little clichéd figures of speech will cure all ills? Is that how little I'm worth?'

'I'm only trying to help.'

'Who asked for help?' She hasn't raised her voice and nothing about her hints at upset, but a fleck of froth clings to the corner of her mouth. She must feel it because she reaches for it with the tip of her tongue, misses and finally wipes it away with the tip of her thumb. 'What are you even doing here, anyway? You should be with your wife. Why did you even ask to meet me here?'

'I have good memories of this spot, this bench.' He clears his throat. 'My wife and I used to come and sit here. It's a good place for lovers, and the long grass is nice for children. There are always grasshoppers in the long grass on warm days.'

Her response is to draw away again. The small family of ducks, a green-necked mallard, a tawny second and a few scuttling chicks, slip in casual diagonals from bank to bank.

'Odd little creatures,' she says. 'Don't you think? They look to be at such peace. But they're not. They're swimming. They have to work to stay afloat.'

From the inside pocket of his jacket, Nick draws out a small brown envelope. He looks at the side of her face, and the sweep of her neck and her bare shoulder, then opens the envelope, withdraws a small bundle of photographs and starts to slowly shuffle his way through them. She steals a glance, and when he doesn't react, leans in.

'What are those?'

'Photographs.'

'I know that. Christ. What do you think I am?'

He sighs. 'No. I'm sorry.'

'And there. Again.'

'What?'

'Placating. I'm sick of it. I'm sick of you. All the time, sorry this, sorry that.'

'Well, what would you prefer? Anger? Violence?'

She stares at him, a grin or grimace showing. 'Why can't you say something you actually mean? Something truthful, just for once. At least that'd be real.'

Nick meets her eyes, his temper fraying.

'How would you know what's real? How would you even recognise it?'

'I'd recognise it. Real would be me lying down there in that river until my lungs started to burn and just opening my mouth and letting it all in. What else would you call that, if not real?'

The first photograph is a close-up shot of a child, a boy of three or four, laughing directly into the camera's eye. Studying the picture causes Nick's frame to slacken. He sighs deeply, then after a second or two steels himself and holds up the picture.

'I want you to look at this.'

In response, she turns her face in the direction of the water.

'Lucy!'

She flinches. Her name strikes like a hand to the face. But her composure returns almost immediately, and she considers the photo and after a few seconds accepts it into her hands, holding it as if afraid it will come apart at her touch. But once it is before her she can't ignore it. She brings it closer.

'He has your eyes,' she murmurs.

'And your mouth.'

'Such a smile,' she says, smiling herself. 'So handsome.'

'He'd be seven today. Richard. The sweetest boy. Such a smile is right. All kinds of sunshine. We named him after your father.'

'Richard,' she repeats, beneath her breath. Then her mouth tightens, and she begins to chew on the meat of her lower lip.

'I remember coming out of the hospital,' Nick says. 'The morning he was born. It was as bright as this, and as warm. I remember it as if it were yesterday.'

'Time does play its tricks, doesn't it?'

'You'd been in labour fifteen hours. I called your folks with the news and my heart was beating so fast I almost couldn't speak. And I came and sat right here on this very bench, just watching the river and the butterflies and bees, and listening to the grasshoppers and the sounds of the park. Trying to regain some focus. When I returned to the hospital, you had him at your breast, our son, and for weeks after we'd looked at one another with the same kind of astonishment, with awe for what we'd created, what miracle.'

'No,' she says, still transfixed by the photograph. 'Don't call him that. Miracles give credit to God.'

Nick looks at her, not quite understanding.

'If we credit God for the good then doesn't that also make Him accountable for the bad? For all the horror?'

'I don't know. Life happens. It's not about blame. Can you remember anything at all from that night?'

In response, she reaches for her book and considers the cover creased nearly to ruin, a lurid science-fictional fusion of oranges and reds with a name once embossed in some brighter colour, white or silver, long since rubbed away from having passed through so many hands. 'Imagine,' she says, speaking seemingly to herself, 'if there's *not* life out there. Think about how terribly lonesome knowing that would make us. It would be almost unbearable.'

'Lucy. Will you at least try? The night. Tell me what you remember.'

With the same steadiness, she hands him back the photo, pushing it away from herself. And she closes her eyes.

'Can you please stop talking? Please?'

She opens her eyes again, meeting his.

'Lucy, we have to face this.'

'No, we don't,' she says, and all at once her expression falters. 'We don't have to do anything. We can just sit here in the sunshine and watch the ducks. And stop calling me Lucy, okay? I'm not who you think I am or who you want me to be. Enough with the names. I'm nobody. Not any more. Can't you get that into your head? I'm nothing. I'm not alive, I'm not dead. I'm nothing.'

'And is that what you think he'd want? What happened was the stuff of nightmares. Children aren't supposed to die. And yet it happens every day. And there was a night, two and a half years ago, when it happened to us.'

'Christ. Go back to placating.'

'What?'

'I asked you to please stop talking. Just shut up and let me sit here. Let me have the sun, and the peace and quiet.'

He knows that she is trying to hold the pieces of herself together, and for a minute or more he says nothing. He looks again at the photographs in his hands and bunches them together, bringing neatness and resolve to their corners.

'This isn't going to work,' he says. 'I can't keep doing it.'

'Who asked you to?' Nothing shows on her face, not a single crease of emotion. Her eyes regard the river as if it is something to be read.

'Do you feel nothing?' he asks. 'Are you so closed off that not even his photo can get to you? Because if that's true then there's no hope. All really is lost.'

'It is,' she says, with something like pity in her voice. 'And it's been lost a long time. You're the only one who couldn't see it.'

She reaches for his hand then, lays their palms flat to one another, hers on top, and knits their fingers together. They sit that way for a while, each caught in their own trap of thoughts, until she raises his hand, turns it over and begins kissing his knuckles. The fact that he is still wearing his wedding ring brings a hint of a smile to her mouth but it hardly shapes itself before dropping away, and she releases her grip on him, gets to her feet, picks up her book and walks off, keeping to the path that follows the flow of the river downstream. From the bench he watches her go, until she is lost to one of the tree-lined bends, and he is left alone.

# Fine Feathers

Every morning, since back when summer first began to turn, our garden is visited by a pair of magpies. The room I use as an office is at the back of our house, on the ground floor, and my desk sits beside a large west-facing window looking out onto a sloping, well-managed garden, with the open land beyond framed by distant hills. I have long since learned that, if I am ever to get anything worthwhile done, routine is essential, and so by seven I'll be in my chair, even on weekends, with a mug of hot tea at my elbow and the scribble-filled pages of whatever manuscript I am working on spread out before me.

The sight of birds lifts my heart. It's difficult to explain, even to myself, and when I've tried to speak of it with Jennifer I have always come up short. It has to do with their colours and how, even among the flower beds, they bloom in ways entirely their own. When grounded, a bird's life seems to jolt between one state and the other, shuffling in small stabs between points of utter stillness, a strictly pendulum existence with each end of the swing distinct in and of itself. Such simplification appeals to me at least as much as their elegance in flight.

I'd been putting out bread and seeds for the smaller ones, the finches, robins and blue tits, and then these black-and-white pests began showing up and devouring whatever crumbs I had spread across the lawn. My initial instinct was to chase them away because I had them down in my mind as filthy carrion, disease-ridden scavengers. I used to feel the same about crows, until I thought about it and understood that we all need to live, even the ugliest of us. And until I took to actually *seeing* them.

The first few times I opened the window to startle them into flight, but by the fourth or fifth sighting I found myself actually anticipating their arrival. Up close, they are such beautiful creatures, not really black and white at all, or not just those stark shades, but possessed of a far more subtle iridescence. The pair that visit my garden are mates. It's not even about affection between them, though there are demonstrations of that, in certain small ways. Their bond is revealed by how comfortable they are together, and how wholly accepting they are of that. And my observance is limited to what they elect to reveal. It might be my garden, but that entitlement stretches only so far. These birds inhabit their own dimension, but they are united in doing so. Sometimes, one will perch on a fence or tree limb while the other forages among the shrubs at the far end of the garden, but even when apart they still seem somehow connected, as if they are seeing from the same eyes, feeling the trembling of the air through the same set of feathers.

Birds don't have it easy, but at least their reasons for dread are more defined. Predators, hunger and the cold. Reducing existence to that makes a black-and-whiteness of life and death. In some ways, people aren't so different, though of course in others we're leagues apart. We lack their sense of unity.

Usually, if Jennifer and I are returning from somewhere together after an evening out, at the theatre, say, or for dinner or drinks with friends, I'll use my door key. Though she has mislaid hers probably no more than three or four times in the six years that we've been living in this house as man and wife, she can never seem to put a hand on it when she needs to, and there's always such a rigmarole of rummaging through handbag and coat pockets that it's just easier for me to be the one who lets us in. On summer nights this is not an issue, and sometimes I am even content to stand and wait while she goes through her motions, but if it's cold or if there's rain or sleet in the air, or the threat of snow, as there is tonight, it doesn't do to linger. The ritual is that, while her fingers continue to fumble through her clothes and other hiding places, I'll unlock the door and step back so that she can enter first. The gentlemanly thing to do. Good manners. Also, making sure that she'd be first in the firing line were we ever to disturb an armed intruder. I've chanced this gag more than once, unable to resist, it being the thing to say that comes so easily to mind, and she laughs, the same way each time, a little croak that rises from no greater depth than the back of her mouth, and slaps a hand against my chest with the same feigned annoyance, leaving me to wonder whether she is playing along out of duty or because she has become so tuned out to my quips that their originality or otherwise no longer even properly registers.

Tonight, though, we're past games. I get out of the car with my key already in hand, and I open the door and go straight through into the kitchen, abandoning her to fend for herself, a challenge to which she has proven more than capable. The line of questioning that I'd started in the car hangs between us. Not the first words I'd thrown at her during our drive back, but the first in the last three or four miles, since before we'd escaped the town limits. There's just something about driving at night on country roads, even roads you've come to know well, that encourages introspection. The tightness of them, and how close they bring you to danger in the darkness, with their sudden bends and their unwillingness to accommodate anything more than moderate speed. A hard, distracted swerve would put us in a ditch, or into one of the low walls or, worse yet, a tree, if I were to line us up just right.

We're sponges, really. We soak up everything that happens, everything that's said and done and everything we see and hear, and we hold it in our hearts. And that can be a lot to bear. Ignorance is too often the better and easier bliss. Details barely registered in the moment have this peculiar and disquieting way of resonating later on, and to live again when we set our minds back on them, each a colour or a brushstroke, however minimal, in the portrait or landscape that we paint.

Opening the door and coming through the hallway is one of those moments that lives on. I've held the sensation of the house's warmth in my face, and also the chill of the outer night against my neck and the back of my head. I carry one along with me, in my wake, even as I plunge into the other. Maybe this moment remains so vivid among all the details of the evening because it captures the whole business in microcosm: desperate suddenly for the sanctity of home, traversing the chasm between what's gone and what awaits, a headlong charge into the fiery future and a bitter reminder of how frozen everything within the past has become.

Even the things we can't rightfully know remain inside us once we learn of them. Maybe those, most of all. We supply the details. The mind's eye fashions the worst possible scenarios and outcomes into lurid being. Nothing can heighten reality like the imagination. And in our heads, in this situation, we spare ourselves nothing. The suffering of it becomes our drug, our high, and we wallow in the torment.

'Stop asking that,' she'd said, her voice from the passenger seat close to tears as I'd taken us up the final stretch of road towards our home. 'If you keep on, I'll tell you. But if I do, you'll want to die.'

I have that moment in me too, but for all that pain, all the tidal visions that accompany her words, there is still, despite everything, the thrilling sensation of having her there beside me, she the all-time beauty to my eyes, trembling inside a dress far too light, low-cut and bare-armed for this weather and this time of year but perfect for a party and the heat of a crowded living room, and for parading before hungry eyes. Silk, of a shade of red that at this hour is just another shadow. Like blood in a black-and-white movie. I held on to what she said and just drove, teeth clenched and barely breathing, keeping the heat of my thoughts, the inferno of them, concealed and my stare nailed to the twenty or thirty yards of road lit by the low spill of our headlights.

Considering it now, I can see how turning my back on her in the hallway might seem symbolic. But leaving her to, as I say, fend for herself, feels like the more apt symbol this night. She looks vulnerable, a slim collage of straights and angles, skin fine as frosting, with a pallor that absorbs the surrounding shades. *Ethereal* is the word I want, or at least the closest I can think of to fit my needs. But looks can so wickedly deceive. She is all the things I've listed, but not just them. Those fine bones are hard as tree limbs, and that delicacy is a trap, a lure. Of course, I know I'm not blameless in what has happened, because I saw only what I wanted to see, and it could be argued, if she were of a mind to do so, that in this way I'd pushed us towards our brink. But misreading is easy when the signs are leading you on, and it's human nature to project, and to fall in love with fantasies. We're all guilty of that, I think, which is why we probably deserve the pain that revelation brings. We set ourselves up for the drop, and fair is a place where they judge pigs and pumpkins. When it comes right down to it, I'd asked to be deceived, or had at least enabled her in her treachery, though there can be no question either that she wore her mask well. And now I am left with the pieces of a broken life.

I hear her steps behind me, the clip of her heels coming down like dropped coins across the hall's Tigerwood parquet, and the front door closing. Not slamming shut but achieving the same effect. Neither one of us thinks to switch on a light, which is probably just as well. The dark is better, because we each look ugly with shame. I pull a chair away from the table and sit with my back to the window. I know where everything is, and yet the kitchen feels unfamiliar. When one certainty fails, everything else loses its standing. After the tapping of Jennifer's heels, the quiet that opens up is deep. She hesitates in the doorway, and her presence is enough to shift the equilibrium. I lift my head, feeling as if I am under water. As my eyes adjust, the lines of the kitchen counter suggest themselves, and it must be the same for Jennifer because this is what she feels her way towards, leading with an outstretched hand. Her silhouette perches on one of the counter's two high stools, but only as a gesture, leaning rather than sitting and keeping her feet on the ground. There's actually nothing to see; so much of this detail can be real only in my mind, and yet it feels no less true for that. I've simply filled in the blanks from what I know.

'Tell me what you're thinking.'

I clear my throat. 'I'm trying hard not to think.'

'That doesn't answer the question.'

The words cause her voice to crack, but that's an old trick. Another show of weakness, vulnerability, but another tool for gaining leverage.

'No.' I have never felt more broken. 'I suppose it doesn't.'

Her hand is resting on the countertop. I know this because, after a few seconds of silence, her fingertips thrum a single rolling arpeggio into the white marble. The sound is minuscule, flesh and just the trim of nail against the cold stone, yet I identify it without hesitation or doubt.

That's how well I know her. We've been living together a long time, and I know the chocolate thumbprint birthmark high up on the inside of her right thigh, and the muffled whine she makes when our lovemaking reaches a height, head rolled back and lips pursed, and I know the feel of her foot in my hand, that small, cool, fleshy cupful of bones, when she has me massaging her after a long, tiring day spent in heels. These details, I have off by heart. It's the bigger things I fail to notice.

'Would sorry mean anything now?' she asks, in the same fractured voice.

I hitch my shoulders and let them relax, at once trusting that she'll sense the gesture and not caring a damn whether she does or not. 'I don't know. Maybe. But it's best, I think, that you don't say it.'

'Why? What's wrong with saying I'm sorry?'

'There's nothing wrong with it. But I'd rather you didn't. Because it wouldn't be enough, and it'd just add to the list of things that I can't or won't let myself believe.'

And now, across the room, tears do come. I sit there and let her cry, forcing myself to listen. The sound hurts me in the way it always has, the few times I've heard it, and for a second I am almost someone else again, the man that, up until a few hours ago, I used to be. But since then I've become the rocks that waves wash over.

'You hate me, is that it?' she asks, when she can.

'Yes,' I whisper. 'Tonight I do. But I hate myself more. Christ, I should have put his head through a wall. If I had any kind of balls I'd have done it. I could feel him watching me, you know? And smirking, the whole time. That mouth, those big doughy lips. I can't make sense of it, how you could bear him, how you could have him on you and actually want it.'

'I told you, Jack. Don't think about it. You'll do yourself no good.'

'Do you have any idea of what you've done, though? Are you even capable of understanding? And the whole bloody room knew. I could see it in people's faces.'

For a second she is angry, like she wants to shout at me, or get up and beat me with both fists. 'For you that's the worst of it, isn't it? Not what I've done but that everyone should know about it.'

I slam my hand down on the kitchen table, and am startled by the magnitude of its noise, which the dark amplifies to the sound of a gunshot.

'You don't get off so easy,' I tell her. 'Not tonight. Stop trying to simplify me, okay? I have a right to anger. If anyone has, I have. And don't think I'm not blaming myself for it, either. Because I am. The signs were all there. If I'd had my eyes put out with a hot poker I couldn't have been more blind. You, joining a book club. I mean, of all the excuses. You don't even fucking read.'

A word more would be an earthquake and the ground already feels unstable. The silence in our home is a void, as crushing as deep space. I blame myself for that, too, because marriages are built for a purpose. For some, that's everything. We've acted casual about it, but it's down to me. Unless a doctor insists otherwise, it's always on the man. We never exactly lacked for effort, but I should have tried harder. Six years is a long time.

We sit here now, miles apart. Nothing moves in the darkness, and perhaps that is why my mind torments itself with pictures of her getting up, moving out into the middle of the floor and slowly unfastening the zip that runs from just beneath her left armpit down to the jut of her hip, so that the red dress can spill away to pool around her high-heeled feet. There's really nothing at all to see, or even to sense, yet I picture her in naked silhouette, as true and honest as anything I've ever known, standing there half turned away, defined by the elegant line of her back in profile, the curves of her breasts, bottom-heavy and slightly upturned. A body moulded to be touched, the waxy smoothness of her skin and the intimacy of her bones pressing cold and alive through the flesh. There to be touched, but not by me, not now and, depending on what the next few days will bring, maybe not ever again. These visions come to taunt me, of course, and to punish. In fact, Jennifer remains at the counter, perched on her stool, not moving and not having moved a hair. The night is packed with uncountable realities.

Finally, when I can bear this no longer, I get up and leave the room. As I go, I seem to know that she is crying again. I feel like crying, too, but tears won't come. I get the hollowed-out feeling of grief, but something inside has run dry, and if Jennifer is crying then I envy her the release. Because of it, though, I almost stop in the doorway. I waver. What has happened, what she has done, is a treachery as bad as any I can imagine, and the details I can't help but attach to it multiply its horror, because that's how the mind works. But people survive worse. Betrayal is such a poisonous act, and it's a question of wanting to find a way on from it. The shards of what has been broken are scattered all around, but perhaps they have not yet been ground into our foundations. Plenty of couples have gone through similar. You piece things back together as best you can, and learn to live with the cracks. You decide how much you can lose, and how much you can bear. That's what it's really all about: deciding. And putting a number on it, quantifying pain and measuring your threshold. We're each of us our mistakes as well as our virtues.

'I am sorry,' she murmurs, to my back. 'Even if you don't want to hear it, or believe it, I am.'

I don't answer, and I suppose she can't be sure if I've even heard. But the words mean nothing. Everyone is sorry when they've been caught. That's not the same as being sorry for what has happened, the act itself and the deceit of trying to keep it concealed, and it's nowhere near enough. Out in the hallway I check the lock on the front door, slip the chain in place and snap shut the deadbolt. Securing the nest. Tonight, all my fears are inside this house, and they live with me, but I still go through the usual motions. If I am honest with myself, I'll acknowledge that this is how our marriage has always been. Love's got nothing to do with it.

# Last Christmas

On the Carrigaline Road, coming onto Carr's Hill, traffic had slowed to a crawl. It was Christmas Eve, already after six, and full darkness had taken hold. Having made a promise to get home early, today of all days, I'd spent the afternoon trying to close off a particularly convoluted account, but because the phone kept ringing I was still the last one out of the office.

The rain of earlier had stopped, giving the roads a sheen inside the headlights, and outbreaks of sleet were forecast for later in the night, possibly turning to snow on higher ground. In the car, with the heat turned up, I moved through the radio's channels, but nothing held my interest and I settled finally on a live choral performance of traditional carols, fixed the volume to an unobtrusive level and tried to relax.

Beside me, on the passenger seat, lay a small palm-sized parcel, wrapped in heavy gold paper and neatly ribboned. My wife's Christmas gift. A month or so ago, when I'd broached the subject of shopping, Angie had suggested that we forgo presents this year, because we were saving for a deposit on a house and really couldn't afford the extravagance. Our plan was to rent for another year at least, and give the market a chance to settle. I shrugged and agreed, even though I was already, since early October, tied into a casual weekly instalment plan on a beautiful quarter-carat diamond and crushed sapphire pendant necklace that I'd seen in the window of the jeweller's on Castle Street. What she'd said made sense, but I didn't want the first Christmas of our marriage to pass without some kind of gesture. And I knew how it would go. We'd argue but she'd be secretly happy. We'd argue, but then she'd lift her hair for me and ask that I fasten the clasp, and she'd admire the way it looked in the mirror, with me at her shoulder, and we'd kiss and make up. Because these are the kind of games we play.

After a few minutes, I cleared the brow of the hill and saw the reason for the delay. Some fifty yards ahead, just at the turn-off to Hilltown, a collision had taken place. One of the cars had run up onto the roadside verge and, from my distance, looked relatively undamaged, but the other had turned over onto its roof. A fire truck was parked at a diagonal behind the wreckage, obviously a necessary manoeuvre but one that reduced the two-way traffic flow to a single available lane. Inside my car, the only sounds came from the radio, the choir segueing from 'In the Bleak Midwinter' into something unmistakably Latin, the name of which escaped me though I knew the melody well enough to have hummed along with, if I'd so chosen.

The heat built, and after a few minutes I was forced to open the window a couple of inches. The initial flood of outer cold felt good but then, in a lull between carols and through the rumble of car engines, I caught the angry sound of a machine, some sort of an electric saw, and through it, screams. A thin, wet voice, pitched at an angle that couldn't be adult. Ahead of me, the cars again began to move, and I eased forward, into that sound, gaining perhaps twenty yards of road before once more coming to a stop. I could have shut the window, or turned up the music. There are times when denial is the only protection available to us. But I did neither. The choir began to sing one of my favourite carols, 'I Saw Three Ships', the voices in a deft arrangement folding together in a way that seemed to put an echo or a shadow around the words. I closed my eyes and swallowed three or four mouthfuls of air. The machine groaned behind the music, a blade made for shredding metal, and the crying came in gouts, filling every available pore of night. I focused on the music, not attaching anything much to the words but letting their sense evoke something older, the recollection of some bright night spent in front of the television as a child, sipping cocoa and watching George C. Scott as Ebenezer Scrooge stride the sullen, snow-clad streets of London. Music has a way of attaching itself to particular and apparently random moments in time, sealing them into a permanent state. When the song ended I switched off the radio.

Again, the car ahead began to move. I watched it veer right by instruction, but held back a moment, letting a gap open, then crawled another twenty yards until a young woman in a luminous yellow traffic vest stepped in front of me, raising a hand for me to stop. I met her eyes and nodded. Because of the temporary lighting that had been set up I could see that she was chewing one side of her lower lip, and that her cheeks were wet. The accident lay just behind her, with the wrecked car and the assembled rescue units blocking off the entire left lane. Beads of glass littered the road, gleaming with the sheen of the rigged halogens. Two firemen knelt beside the upturned car, trying to brace themselves for the possibility of either a release or a sudden collapse, while a third lay on his back and worked a small hand grinder against some snagged knot of metal. Yellow sparks spun away from the cut, and within seconds the air took on the gun-heavy stench of oxidised steel. A few more uniformed types, police and medics, stood some paces back, watching, wanting to help but not knowing how, wanting more than anything, probably, to run. And to one side, away from everyone, a body lay on the road, covered head to shins in a white sheet. Beneath the low hem, the right foot was bare but the left still wore its shoe, something sleek and low-heeled, with an open toe, the single detail that from my distance helped define gender. And still the screams kept on, fragile, fuelled by terror and probably pain, but maybe also by some understanding.

I considered the car's exposed underbelly, something I'd never seen before, veined and channelled with a criss-crossing of cables and pipes, wheels settled in their cradles. Coming from just the wrong angle, though, the window holes gave me back only darkness, even with the halogens spilling hard over everything in between. For three or four minutes then, I watched the traffic being directed, the young woman conducting with swinging arms the line of cars in the opposite lane. Even shaken and upset, the work had to be done. She had her back to me, and I wondered if she had somebody waiting, if she would come home this Christmas Eve to a happy situation, let her hair down and allow herself to be kissed and held. I hoped so because, even though she was turned momentarily away, my mind refused to surrender the image of her tears.

Something happened then. The grinding sound cut out and the car seemed to slump, or give, and all the men who were standing hurried forward to assist. The cluster of bodies made it difficult to see the details, but it seemed that one of the firemen had been able to wrench open the mangled door. While the others attempted to keep the vehicle from collapsing, the man who'd been on his back crawled part of the way inside. Ahead of me, the young woman had abandoned her traffic duty to watch the scene unfold, and was leaning on the front left corner of my car, the glow of the tamped headlight spilling up across her midriff. The howls that we'd been hearing reduced, gradually, to a softer weeping, and I leaned forward and stared, praying, I think, though not in any conscious way, until a child was lifted from the wreckage, a girl of about six, barefoot in a white bell-shaped dress with narrow shoulder straps that offered nowhere near sufficient protection against this weather. I only caught glimpses of her face, not enough really to set her definitively in my mind, but she had hair almost to her waist and a delicate, spidery body. In the fireman's arms, she appeared unhurt but held her shoulders hitched, the corners of them visible through the spill of hair, as if still braced against an impact. As I watched, I saw her turn her head and stare past the men to where the body lay covered, but then the young woman in charge of directing the traffic stepped across my view and gestured at me to move. I nodded, put the car in gear and let her guide me around the accident site and away.

For a while, the silence felt right but when it became suddenly too much I again switched on the radio. I'd expected something to have changed, but nothing had. The choir was still carolling, 'In Excelsis Deo', 'Adeste Fideles'. The traffic into Carrigaline was heavy but moving, and I listened to the music and watched the footpaths on either side thick with pedestrians, mothers holding children by the hand, idling teens, young women in packs, laughing and full of freedom, with their coats worn open and dressed to catch the eye, probably on their way to the last or merely the latest of the Christmas parties. Ropes of lighting stretched above the road, slightly bellying, the bulbs a staggered order of reds, yellows, blues and greens adding something splendid to the night. Most of the shop and pub windows boasted some shade of the season, too; a bauble-and tinsel-clad tree, a slow-moving half-sized Santa, a Happy Christmas message stencilled to the glass in luminous, artificial snow. I moved through the town and turned right halfway up the hill, to follow a darker road home.

Framed by the living-room window, Angie stood lighting mantelpiece candles. I parked on the road, but kept the engine running because I didn't yet want to lose the music, or interrupt the scene with silence. The coloured lights of our Christmas tree shifted to a set rhythm, giving the otherwise dim room its own kind of movement. We'd decorated that tree together a fortnight earlier, the night after my birthday, and I remember threads of tinsel clinging to her hair and a fleck of glitter that I kissed away from one corner of her mouth when, still warm from our exertions, we settled down together on the settee. That night, in the dancing reflections of the fairy lights, we sat holding hands and sipping mulled wine, knowing that whatever we had was only just beginning. Tomorrow, though, would be a new day, and next week a new year, and we both understood that things could change, whether we wanted them to or not.

On the radio now, a soloist was taking on 'O Holy Night', and I could feel the rest of the choir readying themselves to fall in. But for these seconds there was only one voice, a soft, pure soprano swelling unhurriedly towards an immense climax and then holding that impossible top note for longer than I could ever hold my breath. When I closed my eyes I found only colours, and then, through them, I saw again the twisted metal, the glass like hail across the surface of the road, and the shape beneath the sheet. And somewhere among the highest notes of the music, I heard the screams. That was enough. I killed the engine, locked the car and went inside.

Angie, in a white short-sleeved chiffon blouse with its string-drawn collar a good four inches undone and a wool skirt the colour of French mustard that came to just below the knee, blew out the match she was holding and came and put her arms around me. We kissed, and I caught cider and cinnamon from the shampoo she'd earlier used, as well as a hint of wine on the tip of her tongue, but the stench of the match, slightly sulphurous, lay against everything.

'You're late,' she said, finally slipping free. 'You didn't forget that Brian and Liz are calling, did you?'

'I didn't,' I said, releasing her. 'Sorry. I couldn't get away. It's just been that kind of day. And then the traffic was so heavy.'

She turned to the window, and the long red-stemmed candle set into a chunk of holly-clad beech or elm, and struck another match. The candle's wick took the flame, guttered and steadied, and a bright sheen spread across the windowpane, sealing us off from the world. Her feet were bare on the taupe carpet, and I tried not to stare but couldn't help myself. Even after eight months of marriage her details continued to astound me.

I dropped down onto the settee, and held a hand out to her. She looked at me, but remained out of reach.

'I need to get something into the oven. Liz always puts on such a spread.'

'Just for a minute,' I said. The fairy lights made her seem restless. 'They'll be late. I told you. The traffic is heavy tonight.'

With reluctance, she came and sat beside me on the settee. I put my hand to the small of her back, but she either ignored it or had already grown so used to my touch that she did not react. I could feel the bones of her through the chiffon, and it was in my mind to mention the accident but something about the serenity of the room and the stillness of the moment made me hold my words. And happy, I suppose, or at least content, we sat there together for a minute or more, watching the tree, the lights, the soft burn of the candles. Then the telephone began to ring, and she stood and left the room.

# A Death in the Family

At sixty-two, I am already old. Brittle as the sticks we used to gather for kindling, voice careful now and full of draughts, skin like hide. There's not much that I can keep down – a boiled potato mashed into milk, a slice of bread and butter, a mug of tea if it has been left to cool. A problem with my stomach. Hospital is occasionally suggested, where I could be more comfortable and properly looked after, but I've heard of abattoirs talked about in the way I think of hospitals, and I've had enough of those places, I've seen what they did to my sister, Annie. Nobody mentions the other word, and I don't want to hear it spoken, but that's what we're all talking about in our silent ways. So instead of doctors, nurses and a bed in some white room, I take pills crushed into powder, and the odd glass of brandy and sugar, and that's all the treatment I'll allow. Pain or not, I'm fine where I am, for however long that will be. I am inside, shielded from the rain and cold, I have a nice fire, a couch that is comfortable enough on the nights I can't make the stairs, and my daughter and her husband doing what they can, which is more than should rightfully be expected of anyone. And I have my grandson, Billy: six years old, as naturally feral as any cat and the apple of my eye. This is a place I know by heart, having taken my first breath in the little roadside cottage not thirty yards from where I sit now and where my older sister, May, still lives. The place where we were all born and where most of us died, going back to my own grandmother.

Billy is full of questions, full of interest in the stories I tell. He loves to hear about ghosts, fairies and the banshee, and the Black and Tans, and about my father, who'd fought in the Boer War and who, as a way of putting food on our table, had enlisted again, in settled middle age, when the fighting broke out across Europe. Billy sits at my feet, his small, curious fingers plucking at the buckles of my shoes, and listens, head inclined, eyes the wide, ash-blue colour of cloud in storm, while I speak of the things my father told me. Of the officers in Africa who'd wept over the horses that they were forced to leave behind, and how after boarding a boat for home, they'd watched some of those same beautiful animals wade out into the tide and swim, neighing screams through the white wake in desperate rage against the separation, swimming until finally, half a mile out to sea, exhaustion turned meat to lead and the only mercy left was for the sobbing men to draw their pistols from their buttoned holsters. Or of the day back during the Civil War when there'd been fighting on the outskirts of Douglas, up in Moneygourney and along the Passage Road, and May, then only about the age that Billy himself is now, had stood at the little gap in front of our cottage and shouted 'Up de Valera and up the IRA!' as the soldiers marched past. In response, one of the men, a hard-faced fellow with shorn red hair and his clothes caked in mud, picked her up and carried her through the village on his shoulders, which sent the heart crossways in my mother because the soldiers were dressed rough and plain and there was no way to tell whether they were one side or the other, whether they'd celebrate or be offended by the child's cheer. From the floor Billy listens to every word, not smiling but transfixed, and even though some of what I say may not be strictly suitable for the ears of one so young, he doesn't seem to mind.

The past has become close enough to taste, to make a shape beneath my touch. Some mornings, I rise up out of sleep and find myself braced for the long-ago woollen mill's early hooter to rouse the first shift's workers, and tightly tuned to the remembered sense of a body next to me, a husband who has been missing from my bed almost twenty years now. I hear voices in my head, and if they are simply memories rather than ghosts then I also think they share an essence. Time passes but doesn't get far, and maybe for some of us, for those of us nearing our own precipice, the dead still sing.

Lately, I suppose because I have such a willing young audience but probably also because I have begun to see ends in everything, I can hardly stop thinking about Jimmy, the youngest of my brothers and the closest to me in age, who died as a child, a boy of just eleven. I'd glimpsed death prior to his passing, with neighbours or the family members of friends, because in a village as close-knit as ours, at that time, the unravelling of every stitch was felt. But Jimmy was my first experience of death up close and as an overwhelming thing. I watched it come, and linger, and I saw the hole it left behind. And so many years later, on the other side of a lifetime, it's all still there, barely a turn of the head away. In pieces, so that the story can be compressed, because nothing back then happened fast, but in detail so vivid and resonant that the world around me now feels dulled by comparison. And this is the time to remember.

Jimmy was the wildest one of us. We were probably all wild, but while age tamed the rest of us, or took us in different directions, he seemed only ever fully alive when running, or clambering up a tree in search of birds' eggs or chestnuts, or walking in tottering baby steps, arms outstretched, across the top of some crumbling wall. Looking back, I see that he was born for boyhood, that it was not for him merely a passage but the destination. There are some like that, with appetites only for the sweet. And forever trailing in his wake, Puck, his pet goat and constant companion, a patchwork creature all spindle-limbs, short-curled horns and grinning, bleating face.

*

The day leading up to his death was among the longest and most terrible I've ever known. When you are young, waiting is a kind of torture. Our cottage had two rooms to house eight of us, a living room with an open fireplace and a sliver of bedroom, yet on that day we each felt divided by miles and about as alone as it was possible to be. There was just so little to be said. Jimmy had moaned and wept in pain through the previous day and finally lost consciousness some time during the night, and while he curled on his side in the bed by the window, breathing in strums, we'd all either sat or lain awake, afraid of the silence but more afraid of breaking it, certain that a finish was near. My father and mother perched on hard chairs at his bedside; my sisters and I, just paces away behind a dividing curtain, huddled together on our shared pallet bed, holding hands and trying hard not to meet the shine of one another's eyes; and through in the living room, the boys, Dixie and Mata, who had to be up early for work in the Mill, stretched out by the fire.

In the morning my father stood in the middle of the living room. He'd taken Jimmy's accident badly and the previous few months had seen a hard change in him. His skin had greyed to match his thinning hair and begun to hang from his bones, and his eyes were always now a second or two late in finding their focus. Seeing him standing there in the room, shirt half unbuttoned and trousers held up by their braces, I had the impression of a tree about to fall, that same slow, inexorable lean. Annie had water boiled and pressed a mug of tea into his hands, and he looked at it and at her and started to drink in quick, soundless sips, hardly registering its heat.

When he finished, he handed back the mug and went through again into the bedroom, and some minutes later my mother appeared and settled in the armchair beside the fireplace. It was a cold morning, and the fire had yet to properly catch, and we all sat around, watching the small blue and yellow flames bubble among the hazel sticks and the broken clods of turf.

Some months earlier, towards the end of summer, Jimmy was over along the Churchyard Lane, plucking ivy from the old high wall of the Protestant graveyard for the goat to eat. They'd quickly cleared the little that could be reached from ground level and, in order to access the thickest clumps, he climbed up onto Puck's back and then raised himself to standing height. Gripping the wall with one hand and with the other trying to tear loose the fronds of ivy, he had no way of keeping his balance once the goat reared, and was pitched backwards, landing badly on the low kerb separating footpath from road.

I don't remember if Jimmy spoke of it later, and I know for certain that my father never mentioned it, but even if one or both of them had, words are not pictures and have no way of accounting for how clearly the scene plays out in my mind. I sometimes wonder if it was because we shared the same blood, and if kin might be connected in ways that nobody can yet quite understand. I was not there, but they were, and that seems to have been enough, because I can feel the colour of the day and the leathery skin of the ivy leaves, and I can see the goat, unable to bear such a burden, jolt in pain, and Jimmy, for that second flailing in search of balance, one hand scraping at the wall, the other ripping away a swathe of ivy, the leaves waxy and burnt yellow from a long summer, the ropy tendrils dry and weak. And then hitting the ground, hard enough to jerk the breath from his small body, and seeing only soft blue emptiness above the mesh of the graveyard sycamores. A cracking sound, loud as the crunch of a dropped egg, followed after some hesitation by the cautious press of Puck's damp muzzle against his ear and neck; and, in response to his bladder heaving itself empty, a bubbling of tears, driven by fear and shame, to rupture clarity.

Minutes or an hour later, the sound of boots pounding the road at a run, and my father crying out from yards away, throwing himself down onto his knees, afraid to touch and yet in the same instant swallowing Jimmy up into his arms, against his chest, asking over and over, 'Oh Christ, lad, what have you done to yourself?' even while sighing assurances that everything would be all right, that boys were forever falling off walls and out of trees and were always up again and running races in no time flat. But his jarring stare told a different story, because he'd made it through the fighting at Modder River, Loos, Flanders and the Somme, and knew by sense and smell the wounds that were likely to heal and those that wouldn't.

The back was broken. John Looney, a bonesetter from Shanbally and a cousin of my mother's, came to the house, but there was nothing to be done. 'Leave him be, Mary,' he said, outside on the road. 'He couldn't have fallen worse. Give him the bed, and leave him be. He'll do no better in a hospital. All you can do is sit and talk to him, hold his hand. You won't have him long. Months, I'd say. Maybe half a year. But not much longer.' My father stood beside my mother, clenched with rage, eyes dry from pondering space, hating the certainty of the truth.

And the bonesetter knew his business. Within weeks, Jimmy's condition had deteriorated to the point where he was in constant pain. He tried to remain upbeat but the strain had begun to show and on the worst days he could only speak in hisses. By the new year his spine had bent him into a foetal curl, a contortion that forced him to sleep in what was almost a sitting position, propped up with coats and chair cushions. Worse still, if worse were possible, something had got into his bones, a festering that caused him to cry out in the night at the least wrong movement, and it was hard on everyone, having to watch, having to live with that, and to see him suffering so much.

Because there was nothing else that we could do to help, we gave our time, taking turns to sit with him and Puck, whose stubbed head rested on the mattress beneath his hand. I suppose the variety of the conversations kept him going, the boys, Dixie especially, rambling on about hurling or drag hunting or the road bowling up in Scairt, and Annie bringing in all the news and gossip from the Mill, about who was fighting or doing a line with who in the village. May could hardly be near him without crying, but she took her turns the same as the rest of us and would perch on the end of the bed and, with her eyes closed, sing all the songs she knew for him, 'The Old Rustic Bridge by the Mill' and 'The Coast of Malabar' and 'The Stone Outside Dan Murphy's Door', tears lathering her smooth, round cheeks. She had a voice like a bird in those days, and loved to sing almost as much as he loved to listen, though he'd have pretended otherwise.

And for me it was a pleasure, if a sad one, to be able to sit with Jimmy, to discuss the horses that Mr Jago and some of the other men brought to the forge, and how they'd often come across to Jimmy's window for a chat and to ask if there was anything he wanted or needed from the city the next time they were in.

'I can look for nearly anything,' he'd tell me, and I'd nod, having heard him often enough from the other room. 'Maybe a few sweets, sir, if it wouldn't be too much trouble. The nice ones that you brought me a couple of weeks back. If they still have 'em. I have a fierce appetite altogether for bullseyes. And if you ask them for a bit of brusk, they'd probably throw it in for nothing. Sure it's only the dust of the broken sweets, but you'd love the way it crackles in your mouth. God, that's some beast you're after bringing in to the forge there, Mr Jago. You'd nearly need a ladder to be getting up into the saddle. A hackney, is it? He's mighty, but I'd say a devil for throwing shoes. I wonder did anyone ever write a book about horses, at all? I'm stone mad altogether for reading, you know. Especially books with loads of pictures. I don't even mind if they're drawings.'

He had such a roguish way of grinning, a mischievous, gap-toothed innocence that always made me want to play along and to adore him all the more. Because lifting his head was becoming increasingly difficult, he'd twist himself so that he was seeing me from at least one eye, and the near corner of his mouth would lift, dimpling his left cheek, until there was nothing for me to do but smile back and melt for him. And if I ached in those moments to coat his cheeks in kisses, then I was also battling the urge to flee, to run out into the Hall Field where I could throw myself down in the long grass and weep without being seen.

In the months since his fall he'd gathered a decent library of books, two dozen or so, which he kept in a small plywood crate at the foot of his bed. Picture books of dogs, birds and horses, novels like *Peter Pan*, *The Jungle Book*, *Tom Sawyer* and *Treasure Island*, books about the Wild West and Africa, even a book of ghost stories that he'd sometimes read aloud to us so that he could laugh and tease us when we at least pretended to be terrified.

Whenever my mother had a few free minutes, and whenever she could bear it – which wasn't often, though she was a strong woman in most other ways – she'd take up one or another of the books, usually *The Wind in the Willows*, it being his favourite for the creatures in the story, and especially the sweet pastel depictions of toads, rats, badgers and weasels that lit the pages. In slow, halting fashion, she'd read aloud a random page or half a page, missing as many words as she got and accepting his gentle corrections at every stumble. And after she had finally closed the book again and reached for his hand, letting the gesture take the place of the things she couldn't find to say, he'd mumble a passage from the scene between the Wayfarer and Ratty that he'd pored over often enough to know by heart, though he had over time broken it up and made his own of it: 'For the days pass and never return, and the south still waits for you. Take the adventure, heed the call. 'Tis but a banging of the door behind you, and you are out of the old life and into the new.'

\*

The year ended, and all the talk seemed to be of leaving behind everything that had gone before, the fighting and bloodshed, the dividing politics, and concentrating instead on a good future. Nineteen thirty felt like a fresh start, with room ahead for hope. But such optimism didn't penetrate our walls. The cottage for us had become a purgatory, and the sense of dread lay thick within its shadows. Our voices lowered, even when the living room was full; conversations choked on themselves. My father in particular had become a fraction of the man he used to be. He took to standing in the doorway or, if the rain was coming down, to leaning straight-armed on the windowsill, his trance tied to our little front garden's few square feet of earth and the green stalks of daffodil waiting for their time to flower. I watched his back from across the room, and understood that he was thinking of other days, of those times in his life when stillness meant a shallow grave in strange dirt or, in its own way almost worse, having to spend another night, or an hour, or five minutes more back in the flooded trenches with the steely-sour combination stench of blood, earth and rotting flesh and the relentless screaming of the famished rats and those men whose faces had been shot mostly away. I watched him and wanted to stand with him, to put my arms around him and squeeze until his very bones realised that he was not alone, that we were all broken but broken together. But he had become untouchable.

Against all of this, we had the habit of prayer. We believed, but in a way that never demanded much thought, and when the Angelus bell rang out of an evening we all slipped to our knees and bowed our heads, and let the words come in murmurs as insistent as the stream in a roadside gully after an hour of torrential rain. My mother usually led us, and even my father joined in. He'd watch the rest of us kneeling, and after a moment's hesitation would get down himself on the floor on one knee. He was not a devout man, I suppose because of the things he'd seen, done and suffered in his life, but he'd accepted long ago that there was always prayer, even for someone who hardly believed and even when hope was lost. And to everything a purpose under heaven because, looking back, even though those prayers went unanswered, I can see, or believe, that they did give us something, a certain sense of peace, at least for those few minutes each evening, and a chance to hear and listen to our own beating hearts. Maybe, also, an acceptance of our lot.

Because I wasn't yet ten years old, my memories of the time tend to be snatches of detail, often without context; I was a sensitive child, tuned to tensions and emotional imbalances, but was too young to properly comprehend the notion of cause and effect, or to have an awareness of our lives' inner workings, and I hadn't yet learned to look beyond the borders of a picture. The day the Bishop came to confirm Jimmy, I was at home, having just come in from school. Even now I have no idea whether it was by arrangement of a teacher or the parish priest or at the request of my mother, though it seems that we'd been expecting him, because my mother had even borrowed a strip of carpet for him to walk on. It must have been the timing of the visit that caught us by surprise because the carpet was still standing in a tight roll in one corner of the room, all of the others were away at work, Jimmy was sleeping, and my mother, at the fireside, was peeling potatoes into a large pot of water.

'Oh, Jesus, Mary and Joseph,' she wailed, opening the door to him and throwing her hands to her mouth.

'You poor woman,' he said, struggling to suppress a grin, 'you've called me everything now but Danny Boy.'

My mother stepped backwards, half genuflecting, begging his pardon, and after a second or two he followed her inside, shook her hand first and then mine, then glanced around and made for the fire, to stand in contentment with his back to the flames, gathering in and blocking all the heat. He was a big man, not particularly tall, not compared to my father, and not even all that fat, but large-seeming in girth, his broadness and scale emphasised by the loose, flowing wine-red cape and air of authority. I'd seen him before, though always from a distance, either leading the Eucharistic Procession or on occasion over at the church, usually in the company of some visiting missionary, and this close I couldn't help staring at such a large oblong head, laden with jowls and with the fist of a face buried like a punch in its very centre. The shadowy heft of our living room intensified his pallor and that slight vacancy of those bred with the supernatural in mind, and he drew air in whistles through a piggish nose, and had a small womanly mouth with raw lips wetted every few words by a flash of tongue, as if setting himself to be kissed. But when he spoke to tell us how sorry he was for our family's misfortune, his voice was unfussy and kind, with the melody of a West Cork accent used to smiling through hardship.

'Does the lad understand?' he asked, and my mother could only shrug.

'You wouldn't know with him,' she said, glancing at me and then quickly away, deciding, I suppose, that it wouldn't matter now what I heard because I'd realise soon enough, if I hadn't already. 'He wouldn't say, he wouldn't be that kind, but he's cute as a fox after a hare. He must know.'

The Bishop nodded, and without adding anything else, crossed to the bedroom. My mother followed and I moved too, though I kept behind and made myself small in the doorway.

'Jimmy,' she said, 'you have a very special visitor. This is Bishop Cohalan. He's come to see how you've been getting on.'

The Bishop arranged himself on the room's only chair and stared at my mother until she felt compelled to retreat a couple of steps, though she stopped in the doorway, just ahead of me, and folded her arms across her chest, making clear her intention to stay.

'So, Jimmy,' he said, after picking up a book, leafing through it and setting it back down on the bed. 'I heard you'd had a bit of a fall.'

Jimmy had to lean against the windowsill and strain hard so that he could see us. His eyes found me first, and I wanted to smile at him but couldn't, even though I could see that he was afraid.

'I did, Father,' he whispered finally, and the Bishop had to sit forward to catch the words. 'But it was an accident. Don't be blaming Puck for it now, sure you won't?'

'Puck?'

'The goat.' My mother cleared her throat. 'They're great pals altogether, Your Grace. At the end of last summer they were picking ivy off the wall of the Protestant, of the graveyard over along the lane. That's how it happened. He'd climbed up on the goat's back.'

'Oh, I see, yes. Well, don't worry, Jimmy. We won't bother with blame here. As you say, it was an accident.'

'Thanks very much, Father.'

'Tell me, lad. What age are you, at all, now?'

'I'll be twelve in two months.'

'You're a fine man altogether for twelve. And good as gold too, your mother was telling me. Well, most of the time, anyway.'

He paused then, and his expression grew serious, thoughtful. Jimmy watched, in his awkward, low-slung way, but sensing the shift in mood, didn't interrupt.

'The truth of it is, lad,' the Bishop said, at last, 'I'm after a bit of help.' He hesitated again, started to say something else but seemed uncertain how best to continue. 'You see, Jimmy, there's this army I know of.'

'An army?' From where I stood, I could see Jimmy's eyes widen, intrigued.

'Yes. But the problem is, they're in need of a captain to lead them.' This time, the pause was pure theatre, and as much for our benefit as for Jimmy's. 'These last few years, I've been on the lookout for somebody of officer material. If they're out there, then they're mighty thin on the ground. And that's why I'm here today. From what I've been told, I'm convinced that I could travel the length and breadth of Cork County and not find a better fighting man. But what do you think, yourself? Would you be up to the job?'

As if on cue, new light poured through the small window to flood the room. Jimmy, in the bed, pushed himself forward from the wall so that he was sitting to attention, and even with his head hanging towards his chest, and even though I couldn't see his mouth, his smile reached me from across the length of the bed. And within seconds, I knew that he was crying.

'Of course I would be, sir,' he whispered when he could, his tone hiding everything but wetness. 'I'd be the best captain that army ever had. Sure, I already know how to shoot.'

The Bishop settled back into the chair, as if this news had relieved him of a great burden. 'Thanks be to God, Jimmy. To tell you the truth, and bishops are always meant to tell the whole truth and nothing less, I'm fierce relieved. It's a big job, as you can imagine, and I was beginning to think I'd never find anyone suitable. But that's grand, so. There's just a few prayers we need to say, and I have to give you a special blessing, and then you'll be all set to lead the angels. They're in desperate need of a good brave man like yourself.'

They prayed then, Jimmy, hands knotted together in his lap, joining in with the words where he could, though he'd never been much for Mass, and mumbling through the rest, hoping I suppose that his mistakes would either go unnoticed or could be overlooked. The Bishop closed his eyes and performed a shortened Confirmation ceremony, and we stood in the bedroom doorway and looked on, wanting to look away.

When they'd finished, the Bishop reached out and shook Jimmy's hand in congratulations.

'You did fine, lad,' he said. 'Your mother's right. As good as gold.'

'Thanks, Father. It didn't hurt a bit.' Jimmy was grinning, too. 'But about that army. When can I go, do you think?'

The Bishop looked at him. 'It won't be long now, lad. Soon enough, I'd say.'

My mother turned away then, the tears turning her steps already blind, and stood in the centre of the living room, too sick in her heart to sit, trying to smother the barking of her sobs with cradling hands. She was still that way when the Bishop rose to leave, and he shook hands with Jimmy again, lay a hand in blessing on his head, then came into the doorway, considered the scene, nodded to himself, and left.

Once he'd gone, I urged my mother into the chair beside the fire. She let herself be led, sat down in a forward lean that pressed her elbows into her knees and, chiding herself for never even having offered the man a cup of tea, continued to weep, but in a quiet way.

\*

The morning of that last day started off grey and mild but by afternoon had thickened with mist, an icy fur that smoked the air and turned everything soft and silver. The cottage remained silent, apart from the muted shuffle of visitors. A couple of times, after morning Mass and then again just as dusk was closing in, the priest; but mainly relatives and neighbours, coming through the door and carrying the dampness on their backs, pressing cold hands into ours, even mine, young as I was, and saying how sorry they were for our trouble.

In the living room we all stood or sat around, May and Annie on the floor beside the settled fire, my mother in the armchair, numb with grief. Dixie and Mata held up the room's corners, restless in their stretching, afraid to disturb the stillness too much, but not knowing quite what to do or where to put themselves. I remained a long time at the window, leaning into the draught just where the wooden frame had separated a crack from the stone and feeling its kiss on my cheek or, when I inclined my head just right, in some thrilling way against the corner of my mouth. The mist felt full of ghosts. Across the way, the forge was doing quiet business, so I only now and then caught the clap of an arriving or departing horse, that heavy yet somehow delicate sound of iron shoes laid down on packed dirt. It was weather for tears but we were all dry from weeks of that, and once the light washed finally from the day even the outline of the road was lost to me. The hedges dulled to silhouette and only the stubs of nearby daffodils remained distinct, their brightness odd now and somehow out of place.

Then the bedroom door opened, and my father appeared. His mouth had tightened to a slit and his eyes seemed fixed on distant things. My mother looked up, teeth clenched between wide-open lips, and it took me a second to understand what she was thinking, and my father even longer. When he did, he gasped, and said quickly: 'He's asleep again. But he's fierce restless.'

All day, Jimmy had been lost in the depths of a bad sleep. The doctor had left medication, a brown syrup that reeked of hops and something like liquorice, and it was just about strong enough to keep him out but scarcely dulled the pain. He moaned and sometimes wept, sitting with his knees folded to his chest, his face even in that unconscious state so twisted with suffering that all trace of boyishness had been stripped back. From the doorway I chanced to look, and saw a monster, not a boy.

On better nights, when a wind was blowing hard in the chimney and we could persuade my mother to frighten us with a ghost story, she'd sometimes talk of the fairies, and how they were constantly watching for the opportunity to snatch an infant and replace it with one of their own, a changeling that by some terrible magic had been made to look identical to the stolen child. The changeling would grow into the family, spreading wickedness and misery, tearing them apart, until another little corner of the world was in ruins. Peering through the doorway now, past the crumbling tower of my father and the spindling, head-slung goat to the narrow bed, it was hard not to wonder whether such stories could have evolved from some raw fact, and whether the desperate, misshapen thing wrestling so viciously with sleep was still the brother I loved or actually something much more terrible.

My mother had told us that in rare cases, once it had achieved its mayhem, the changeling would allow the spell to slip so as to reveal its true form. Now that our family had been ripped to ribbons, I remember thinking, maybe it was finally showing itself to us. I didn't say any of this aloud but, based on the little I'd seen in stealing my glimpse, it was one of the notions that passed through my mind and lingered. Because at ten years old, with night coming down and the easy redness of the fire providing the living room's only light, nothing seemed impossible.

And when, at six o'clock, the dusk was penetrated by the sombre clanging of the church bell, and we all got down on the floor on our knees and followed my mother's prayers to a God who'd either forgotten us or didn't care, the only question I asked myself was why such wicked things as fairies were allowed, even in stories, to exist, while so much good, and all too often the very best of us, had to suffer such bad endings.

We prayed, and the darkness took hold, and we all knew without having to be told that we were in the final hours. Jimmy's breathing was increasingly laboured, rustling like old trees in a hard wind, and if there was terror and sorrow at the thought of that finally stopping, then there was also, to our shame, an undeniable sense of relief.

A couple of hours later he began to call out, in a voice so weak that at first none of us could make sense of the sound. The light of the paraffin lamp made his face a small knot of reefs and shadows, and his eyes were not just closed now but clenched. My mother sat at the bedside, with Puck's chin resting on her knee, my father standing behind her, one hand holding itself in the air, its intent surely to settle on her shoulder in a gesture of support but for some reason unable to make the reach. Seeing this seemed to emphasise the distance that had come to lie not just between them but between us all, and from the other room, huddled among my brothers and sisters, I considered again the twisted figure in the bed, hardly recognisable now even as human, especially in the lamplight, and started to cry.

'It's Sally,' said Mata, after some interminable stretch of time had passed, and he got up from where he'd been sitting and went through into the bedroom. 'He's calling for Sally, I think. That's what it sounds like.'

My father looked at him, barely registering the words, but when Jimmy began to moan again, he leaned forward to make sense of the sound. And Mata was right.

Sally was my mother's sister. She'd never married and lived with her three bachelor brothers in a small, crumbling terraced house a mile or so from us, along the Passage Road. She was a thickset woman in her early fifties, with a gusty and volatile nature, and we had all thrilled to the stories of her diehard actions during the War of Independence, about how she'd fed and sheltered men on the run. Even after the Black and Tans had gone, she continued to carry a loaded pistol, and would brandish it at the least cross word or opportunity to shock. Until Jimmy's fall she'd often taken him with her up into the Heighty Hills or the fields around Moneygourney for a day of target practice, swearing him to secrecy so that my father wouldn't find out. She doted on him, likely resonating to the feral strain in his nature, and she had been here all morning and for long stretches of the previous week, sitting at his bedside, holding his hand, telling him stories, listening while he could still talk sensibly as he explained about the army he was going to captain and the battles he'd soon be fighting.

'Someone will have to go for her,' my mother whispered, her voice sawdust after all the tears.

'Tonight?' Mata stepped back out of the bedroom. 'It's already late, and it's an awful night out.'

'He'll get no peace until he has her here.'

'I can go, I suppose,' my father sighed. He was still standing, and had been for hours, but exhaustion had broken him. His face and limbs slackened, and he looked set to come apart.

My mother turned and took a fist of his shirtsleeve. 'I need you here, Jer. I can't be on my own.'

In the living room, May bowed her head and began to sob, and nobody spoke. And as we sat there Jimmy began to cry out again, and this time, I suppose because we were looking for the shape of the name, we all clearly heard the call. He repeated the cry twice more, a slur of sorrow and pleading, and I felt a tightness across my chest.

'I'll do it,' I murmured, so low that, at first, because nobody responded, I assumed they'd not heard. I cleared my throat. 'I'll go. It won't take me long.'

In the firelight, I caught the sheen of Annie's eyes. Her mouth was tight, but finally she nodded.

'Take my coat. You'll be drenched with that mist.'

No one said anything else. May continued to weep, and the boys kept to the room's corners. From the bedroom my father watched me slip on the oversized coat, but his expression didn't shift.

Outside, the night was colder than I'd expected. I pulled the door shut behind me but hesitated, fastening the buttons of the coat and then folding my arms to keep it tight across my chest. The silence felt immense, the road ahead a wash of drizzle. I braced myself, and strode forward.

My intention when volunteering to go for Sally had been to run, but something about the lack of sound killed that urge. I can't explain it. In the dark, and with the mist obliterating distance and walling me in, I should have been afraid. I knew the road, but never this late and never on my own, and I'd never known it anything like this. It was a night for dead things and yet I felt only a sense of calm, as if there was something protective about the closeness.

I walked the hundred yards or so to the turn-off for the Passage Road, keeping my pace slow, and there was no sense of urgency and no sounds at all except for my own light footsteps and the gentle pull and shatter of my breathing. Then the Finger Post pressed itself into view, a ten-foot post on an anchoring four-foot rubble-and-mortar mound, with three arms pointing out the varying directions, to the city, Passage West and Carrigaline. When Dixie would try to frighten Jimmy and me, he'd tell us about how, back in early times, fifty years before the Famine, the English had hung people from those arms, and it was sung about, and believed by many, that the ghost of a man from Donnybrook named Phil Carty, who'd been strung up there in chains for his part in that long-ago rebellion and left to rot, could still be seen on certain nights slumped against the post's mound, drenched in blood from the beating he'd taken and weeping for the life he'd lost.

Remembering this put a shiver through me, but it was a pleasurable dread, made easy by familiarity, and I laughed into it and kept moving forward. But as I drew closer to the signpost, I saw that the dark held something else.

Set back on the road, no more than a dozen paces away against the high wall, a man stood staring at me. To my child's eyes – and even still, in memory – a giant, comfortably over six foot, because I knew that wall well and he was easily head and shoulders above it. But in the moment, my shocked mind made him probably half as tall again, wrapped in a long buttoned-up overcoat, his marble-white face a forlorn blur behind the sheets of mist.

My bones turned soft. I wanted to cry out, but the air only dribbled from my mouth until my chest burned, and a chill that had nothing to do with the cold of the night ran the length of my spine. Ahead of me the man's stare didn't slip, and even though I could make out very little of his face other than its whiteness I felt helpless and stuck beneath that stare.

There are days even now when I wonder if it was real. Because it's possible, I suppose, that I'd suffered a moment of breakdown, brought on by an accumulation of the darkness, mist, the thought of ghosts and the imminence of my brother's death. Grief does funny things to the mind, and a ten-year-old keeps so much room in the world still for magic. All I can say is that it felt real, and the details have remained with me in a way as rich and vibrant, as true, as any other single moment of my life. It's as real to me as this room around me now, so real that I remember the feeling of the mist against my eyes and the way the man's hair lay buttered to his forehead. The wide fixation of his stare and the sadness it held; the slightly bowed clench of his mouth over the strong chin. Conditions and distance blurred the details, and yet in memory they feel beyond question. The entire encounter could have lasted no more than a few seconds, but shock somehow froze the moment solid, so that it continues to retain its shape, its permanence, the way photographs do. I might have stood there forever had he not moved, but then his mouth slipped open as if to speak, to call or warn me, and a hand lifted from his side, and that proved enough to crack the spell. I came to with a jerk, reared back hard and ran.

Logic would have turned me for home, but in the dark there was no room for that, and no time to think, and I charged westward, following my original plan, down into the black well of the Passage Road, a narrow boreen penned in on both sides by ancient walls and a heavy overhang of oaks and sycamores. I ran blindly, my feet pounding the road, chasing to catch the frantic rhythm of my heart, and when a terrible wailing ruptured the night I began to cry, which caused a further melting of the world, my terror so immense that I'd almost reached Sally's house before I recognised the howls as my own. Even then, though, I didn't stop, couldn't. I ran, certain that the figure was behind me, and that any second I'd feel the grab of a cold hand. Then I took the twist in the road and the row of little homes came into view ahead and on my left, and I didn't slow my pace until the front door stopped me. I beat at the old timber with my fists, and called out in desperate shouts for Sally, and that was almost the worst moment, because I could hear the rising sounds of voices inside, and then the shamble of footsteps, and I was so near to being safe. 'Sally!' I cried, and hammered at the door, and when, finally, it opened into a softer lamplit dark, I tumbled in and flapped a hand behind me at the night. But the road was empty.

They brought me to the fire, which had almost burnt out, and I sat on a hard chair and stared into the embers, weeping for breath. Sally and her eldest brother, Mick, stood waiting, Mick holding the lamp so that they could better see my face in the light. A minute or two later, another brother, Richard, came through from the back of the house in his vest, thumbing his braces up onto his shoulders, his smoke-stained hair corkscrewing up from the top of his head.

'It's Jimmy,' I said, when I could make the words. 'They're saying he mightn't last the night. He's been calling for you, Sal. You'll have to go up to him. Mam says he won't die without you.'

'Christ almighty, child,' she said, kneeling before me and undoing the buttons of my coat. 'You're soaked to the bone. Let me get you dry.' She used a towel on my head, rough in her usual way, then wrapped me in a blanket and pulled me into her arms. I held myself tightly to her neck and began to cry again. The smell of oil from the lamp was strong in the room, but its glow relaxed me. At the fire, behind Sally's back, Richard stooped and added a sod of turf, and a few sticks of kindling, and stirred the rose-coloured ashes with a heavy iron poker. Mick started to say something, but hesitated, set the lamp on the table and left the room, returning after a moment with a bottle and a cup. He poured himself a drink, swallowed it in a quick throw, then lingered over a second.

'There was a man,' I said, when I'd settled back a little in the chair. 'By the Finger Post. A stranger. He was just standing there, against the wall. I got an awful fright.'

Mick put the cup to his mouth again. 'What kind of a man?'

I closed my eyes and the image returned. I shuddered hard. 'Tall,' I told them. 'The tallest man you ever saw. He had on a long grey coat, and he must have been there in the mist for a long time because his hair was clung to his head. His face was the colour of milk, and he had a kind of a sadness about him that you'd nearly feel in your stomach.'

They were all staring now, leaning in.

'Did he say anything?' Sally asked, still on her knees before me.

I shook my head. 'No. It looked like he was going to, but that's what got me running. God, I thought he was behind me the whole road down. My heart is still going a gallop.'

Sally looked across at Mick. He emptied his cup with a hard swallow.

'What?' I asked, confused and again growing afraid. 'Do you know him? The man?'

At first, no one said anything. Then Mick shrugged. 'Maybe. But there's no need to be worrying.'

'But who is he?'

'It sounds like your grandfather,' Sally said. 'Mick is right. You hadn't reason to be afraid. He'd have been there to watch over you, that's all.' She stood, then leaned in again to kiss me on the cheek. 'You can stay here with the lads tonight, and come up in the morning. No sense in you getting soaked a second time. They'll get the fire awake and make tea. The night won't be long going.'

'You're not walking up on your own?' I said, reaching out and gripping her sleeve. 'But it's so late. And supposing he's still there? The man, I mean.'

217

'If he's who I think he is then he won't harm me. And if it's anyone else, sure don't I have my pistol? So that'll be his bad luck. Anyway, I've no fear of the night-time.'

We sat up all night, drinking tea and chatting, I telling them about school and Mick talking about the horses in Windsor, where he worked as a coachman, and about Sir Abraham Sutton, a one-time Lord Mayor of the city but who'd never been the same after burying his only child, a daughter, Miss Kathleen. A beautiful young thing, and as attached to him as his own shadow, she'd contracted tuberculosis while accompanying him on his monthly charitable rounds and within six months had coughed up her lungs and wasted away to nothing but skin. 'The rich die the same as the poor,' he said, emptying the last of the bottle into his cup. 'And money won't spare them the suffering.' The darkness held, but hours had passed and I could feel the dawn breaking.

An hour later, after drinking yet more tea and eating bowls of steaming porridge, Richard suggested that we walk the road back together. The night's mist left behind a raw cold, and the snatches of cloud that revealed themselves through the occasional breaks in the tree branches were as heavily grey as a wintry sea. But the early morning was lit by the racket of birdsong, and as we walked, just for something to say, I made a small game of identifying robins, blackbirds, wrens, sparrows and wood pigeons by their calls, and the two men listened and nodded, though I knew their thoughts were with other things.

When we came to the Finger Post, nobody mentioned what I'd seen, and we quickened our pace, which had until then been leisurely, and turned in to Douglas. And once we got to within twenty or thirty yards of the cottage I felt it, the air of death, and I broke from between my uncles and ran ahead.

The front door was wide open, and our little home was crowded with people. Faces considered me with sad, fascinated eyes, and hands settled in sympathetic fashion on my back. Neighbours mostly, but the priest, too. I looked past the pack of bodies for May and Annie, and saw them beside the burnt-out fire, both of them crying. Dixie and Mata were standing around, isolated with their grief, feeling themselves too big and awkward for the limited space, and trying not to be in the way. I pushed through into the bedroom doorway, and stopped. Sally had my mother in her arms and was whispering something that might have been a prayer, and my father stood above them, his head turned away. There was a clean smell of freshly cut flowers; someone, probably May, had been into the Hall Field to gather the snowdrops and the early primroses. I tried to avert my eyes from the bed, and Jimmy, who was still sitting upright as usual among the pile of coats and cushions, head down and twisted leftwards. But it was impossible not to stare. The scene was one I knew well, and yet everything was different. This, I realised, taking a few steps closer, pushing past Sally and my mother to stand at his side, was death. The silence of it frightened me. The vacancy. I knew the shape, but what remained was a husk, nothing more than flesh and bone. The life inside, the laughter and even the recent agony, was gone. The face, impossibly young-seeming, looked only vaguely familiar, and

I knew even at ten that it was because I'd forgotten the sight of it in a state of ease, with the muscles slackened. I leaned in and kissed his cheek, and the coldness of the skin brought tears to my eyes but I didn't pull away, not until my father put his hands on my shoulders and whispered, 'All right, Nellie, love. That's enough. He's gone from us.'

We'd all been waiting weeks for this end, and now that it had arrived I wasn't ready. I put my arms around him and hugged him tight, and sobbed in his ear that I loved him as much as any heart could and that I always would, that I'd think about him every day and would make sure Puck was fed and watered and well looked after.

My father took charge then. I moved back in answer to his hand, and he straightened up as best he could and cleared his throat.

'Take Mary out into the other room a while, Sal,' he said, his voice so low that I could hardly hear him.

Sally looked up, without seeming to register the words.

'Come on,' he said, with more force. 'Take her out and see to the kids, will you?'

He waited a second, then moved to the foot of the bed and lifted the timber crate of books from their place in the corner of the room.

Realisation came slowly, first to Sally, who gasped, and, after a second or two, to my mother. Her broad face twisted and she began to wail and claw at her hair. 'No, Jer. Please, don't. Not that.' As she begged, her legs gave and she spilt to the floor, but the words and the howling kept on, deep broken sounds that lost all shape yet somehow retained their meaning.

My father's eyes were glass. Focused, I think, on the minutes that lay ahead for him, but probably remembering things, too. His entire adult life, maybe even longer than that, he'd never been more than a few steps away from war. And now, as I looked on, he just stood there, holding the wooden box under one arm, until Sally had lifted my mother once again to her feet, then began to shepherd the women towards the doorway. Ahead of them, I stepped backwards out into the crowd, which parted a little for me.

'Please, Jer,' my mother implored, as he eased her from the bedroom. 'Don't do it.'

I noticed, for the first time and only because of the way he turned and caught the light, that his own cheeks were wet too, streaked in tears. 'You think this is what I want, Mary? But what choice is there? I have to get him straight. If I don't, we'll never fit him in the coffin.' He broke off then, and his right hand gripped the bedroom door a moment, and within the frame, clear from everyone else, he was a portrait of pain, this strong man who must have believed he'd already seen all the horror that life could raise but who was finding himself now on the brink of its most terrible moment yet. His eyes stared without focus, and we all stared back at him without wanting to, because there was nowhere else to look.

When he pushed the door shut there was a long silence, half a minute's worth, maybe more, and then the bestial sounds of him weeping from his chest louder and louder above the dry crunch of breaking bones.

*

Lately, I think a lot about endings. I have no fear of death, but I'd rather not see it coming. Because I've already known enough of it in my life. Some days now are good, and others less so, and on those down-days I can feel it in the air. You just know. The coloured lights and comfortable darkness of Christmas are gone, and February has blown in cold and wet, the rain constantly scratching at the glass. I turned sixty-two only days ago, and everyone came and held my hand and kissed my cheek, but I could only taste a spoonful of the cake they brought, and I let Billy blow out my candles. Since then, since before then, I've had this ache in my throat, of the sort that grown men and women get when they need to cry. And through the longest part of the day, those two or three beaten hours that stretch out from noon, I close my eyes and find again the faces of those who have gone before. And the sense of waiting feels unbearable.

This is how death can be when it's slow in arriving. Time becomes a tide on the turn. You stop wishing and counting days, and start looking at the things you've left behind. While my daughter has gone to collect Billy from school, the house keeps a baited silence, and all the people I've ever been in my life huddle close. In that same instant, I am sixty-two and I am young, a smiling wife and grieving widow, mother, grandmother, millworker, house cleaner, and happy, frightened, broken-hearted child. And in recent weeks, the self that has come to exist most solidly for me is the ten-year-old, the one who stood all those hours in Jimmy's bedroom doorway, who ran the Passage Road for him in the cold rain with a devil or an angel to heel, and who lay awake so many nights straining to listen and cowed to quietness at the thought of death, that first real feel of it, and what it must mean. The passing years are supposed to soften what has gone before, but they don't. Because for most of us, the past has nowhere to go. The best we can do is live beneath its weight.

If I could talk of all this or write it down, then I'd do so, but I haven't nearly the understanding or the eloquence. I am not stupid, but with only a few years of basic schooling and a life lived in meagre ways, I lack the skills, the tools for properly explaining myself. I speak to Billy in my simple way, because he hangs on my words, my voice, and the best I can do is tell him about the things I've seen, learned and been told, and to hold him steady while he straddles ancient worlds. We're as close as clapped hands, he and I, and perhaps, if he is listening carefully, he'll hear what gets told between the lines of what I say, and catch the whisperings of my heart. If we are both lucky or blessed and if it is meant to be, maybe he'll someday find a way of passing them on, to someone else who'll care enough to listen. He'll remember and talk of me and the moments of my life, he'll tell my stories as they're meant to be told, and through them and him I'll get to live a little bit again.

# Acknowledgements

E arlier versions of some of this collection's stories have appeared previously, in slightly or significantly different form: 'The Border Fox' in the *Kenyon Review* and *London Magazine*; 'A Sense of Rain' in *Southword*; 'Wildflowers' in the *Honest Ulsterman*; 'Fine Feathers' in *Agni*; 'Last Christmas' in the *Saturday Evening Post*; 'A Death in the Family' in *Ploughshares*. Additionally, 'The Boatman' was shortlisted for the Costa Short Story Award and appeared in the *Chattahoochee Review*.

I want to acknowledge the Arts Council of Ireland/An Comhairle Ealaíon for the award of a literature bursary, which enabled me to focus on completing this collection at a time when I really needed the support.

My deepest appreciation goes to my editor, Robin Robertson, for giving these stories – and me – a chance in the world. I'll be forever grateful for what has really proven a life-changing opportunity. And this collection was blessed to have two editors, Robin and also Daisy Watt, to put it through their very exacting wringer. Their care and attention to detail has made the book what it is, and hopefully at this stage only the intentional kinks remain.

The writing of a book is just part of the battle, and for knocking it so beautifully into shape and getting it out onto bookshelves and into readers' hands I have to thank all the wonderful and dedicated staff at Jonathan Cape and Vintage. I couldn't wish for better. My thanks also to Jane Kirby, who got the book across the water, and to the team at Harper, and most especially Terry Karten, for showing faith in my writing and bringing my stories to a US audience.

And finally, my love and thanks to my family, for their unending support and encouragement: Martin, Kate, Liam and Ellen; Yann Donnelly; Ying Tai Chang; and my parents, Liam and Regina. Because of them, I'm the luckiest person I know.

penguin.co.uk/vintage